The Firebird

and Other Russian Fairy Tales

Arthur Ransome

Illustrated by Simon Galkin

DOVER PUBLICATIONS, INC.
Mineola, New York

Bibliographical Note

The Firebird and Other Russian Fairy Tales, first published by Dover
Publications, Inc. in 2004, reprints, in slightly edited form, nine stories from
Old Peter's Russian Tales, originally published by T. C. and E. C. Jack, Ltd.,
London, in 1916.

Library of Congress Cataloging-in-Publication Data

Ransome, Arthur, 1884–1967.
    The Firebird and other Russian fairy tales / Arthur Ransome ; illustrated
by Simon Galkin.
       p. cm.
    "Reprints, in slightly edited form, nine stories from Old Peter's Russian
tales, originally published by T.C. and E.C. Jack, Ltd., London, in 1916"—T.p.
verso.
    Contents: Sadko—Frost—The three men of power—Baba Yaga—The little
daughter of the snow—The golden fish—Alenoushka and her brother—
Prince Ivan—The Firebird, the Horse of Power, and the Princess Vasilissa.
    ISBN 0-486-43893-7 (pbk.)
    1. Fairy tales—Russia. [1. Fairy tales. 2. Folklore—Russia.] I. Galkin,
Simon, ill. II. Ransome, Arthur, 1884–1967. Old Peter's Russian tales. III. Title.

PZ8.R174Fi 2004
398.2'0947—dc22

            2004056120

Manufactured in the United States of America
Dover Publications, Inc., 31 East 2nd Street, Mineola, N.Y. 11501

Note

These nine classic fairy tales transported children's imaginations in old Russia, and still do so today. They are filled with magic beasts, daring young men, beautiful maidens, wicked witches and, as might be expected, lots of snow.

In one of the most famous of these tales we are introduced to Baba Yaga, a fearsome witch whose legs are just bone and who has metal jaws and drives a mortar and pestle through the woods. Not surprisingly, she likes to eat children. On the other hand, she can also underestimate their cleverness. The composer Moussorgsky devoted one section of his *Pictures at an Exhibition* to Baba Yaga.

In another tale we catch sight of the magnificent firebird, whose feathers are made of gold. Rising at dawn, it sheds golden light over the forest as it flies. The glorious beauty of a single feather from the firebird changes forever the life of a young archer. The archer also rides a magic horse called a "horse of power" who can gallop mightily and give very good advice. Stravinsky's ballet *The Firebird* is based on this story.

The other Russian classics in this book include "Sadko" and "The Little Daughter of the Snow" (Rimsky-Korsakov wrote operas based on both of these), as well as "Frost," "Prince Ivan," "The Golden Fish," "The Three Men of Power," and "Alenoushka and Her Brother."

The author, Arthur Michell Ransome, lived from 1884 to 1967, and traveled from his native England to Russia, China and Egypt, among other places, collecting folk and fairy tales for his many children's books.

Contents

List of Illustrations

Sadko

IN NOVGOROD in the old days there was a young man—just a boy he was—the son of a rich merchant who had lost all his money and died. So Sadko was very poor. He had not a kopeck in the world, except what the people gave him when he played his dulcimer for their dancing. He had blue eyes and curling hair, and he was strong, and would have been merry; but it is dull work playing for other folk to dance, and Sadko dared not dance with any young girl, for he had no money to marry on, and he did not want to be chased away as a beggar. And the young women of Novgorod, they never looked at the handsome Sadko. No; they smiled with their bright eyes at the young men who danced with them, and if they ever spoke to Sadko, it was just to tell him sharply to keep the music going or to play faster.

So Sadko lived alone with his dulcimer, and made do with half a loaf when he could not get a whole, and with crust when he had no crumb. He did not mind so very much what came to him, so long as he could play his dulcimer and walk along the banks of the little river Volkhov that flows by Novgorod, or on the shores of the lake, making music for himself, and seeing the pale mists rise over the water, and dawn or sunset across the shining river.

"There is no girl in all Novgorod as pretty as my little

river," he used to say, and night after night he would sit by the banks of the river or on the shores of the lake, playing the dulcimer and singing to himself.

Sometimes he helped the fishermen on the lake, and they would give him a little fish for his supper in payment for his strong young arms.

And it happened that one evening the fishermen asked him to watch their nets for them on the shore, while they went off to take their fish to sell them in the square at Novgorod.

Sadko sat on the shore, on a rock, and played his dulcimer and sang. Very sweetly he sang of the fair lake and the lovely river—the little river that he thought prettier than all the girls of Novgorod. And while he was singing he saw a whirlpool in the lake, little waves flying from it across the water, and in the middle a hollow down into the water. And in the hollow he saw the head of a great man with blue hair and a gold crown. He knew that the huge man was the Tzar of the Sea. And the man came nearer, walking up out of the depths of the lake—a huge, great man, a very giant, with blue hair falling to his waist over his broad shoulders. The little waves ran from him in all directions as he came striding up out of the water.

Sadko did not know whether to run or stay; but the Tzar of the Sea called out to him in a great voice like wind and water in a storm,—

"Sadko of Novgorod, you have played and sung many days by the side of this lake and on the banks of the little river Volkhov. My daughters love your music, and it has pleased me too. Throw out a net into the water, and draw it in, and the waters will pay you for your singing.

And if you are satisfied with the payment, you must come and play to us down in the green palace of the sea."

With that the Tzar of the Sea went down again into the waters of the lake. The waves closed over him with a roar, and presently the lake was as smooth and calm as it had ever been.

Sadko thought, and said to himself: "Well, there is no harm done in casting out a net." So he threw a net out into the lake.

He sat down again and played on his dulcimer and sang, and when he had finished his singing the dusk had fallen and the moon shone over the lake. He put down his dulcimer and took hold of the ropes of the net, and began to draw it up out of the silver water. Easily the ropes came, and the net, dripping and glittering in the moonlight.

"I was dreaming," said Sadko; "I was asleep when I saw the Tzar of the Sea, and there is nothing in the net at all."

And then, just as the last of the net was coming ashore, he saw something in it, square and dark. He dragged it out, and found it was a coffer. He opened the coffer, and it was full of precious stones—green, red, gold—gleaming in the light of the moon. Diamonds shone there like little bundles of sharp knives.

"There can be no harm in taking these stones," says Sadko, "whether I dreamed or not."

He took the coffer on his shoulder, and bent under the weight of it, strong though he was. He put it in a safe place. All night he sat and watched by the nets, and played and sang, and planned what he would do.

In the morning the fishermen came, laughing and merry after their night in Novgorod, and they gave him a little fish for watching their nets; and he made a fire on the shore, and cooked it and ate it as he used to do.

"And that is my last meal as a poor man," says Sadko. "Ah me! who knows if I shall be happier?"

Then he set the coffer on his shoulder and tramped away for Novgorod.

"Who is that?" they asked at the gates.

"Only Sadko the dulcimer player," he replied.

"Turned porter?" said they.

"One trade is as good as another," said Sadko, and he walked into the city. He sold a few of the stones, two at a time, and with what he got for them he set up a booth in the market. Small things led to great, and he was soon one of the richest traders in Novgorod.

And now there was not a girl in the town who could look too sweetly at Sadko. "He has golden hair," says one. "Blue eyes like the sea," says another. "He could lift the world on his shoulders," says a third. A little money, you see, opens everybody's eyes.

But Sadko was not changed by his good fortune. Still he walked and played by the little river Volkhov. When work was done and the traders gone, Sadko would take his dulcimer and play and sing on the banks of the river. And still he said, "There is no girl in all Novgorod as pretty as my little river." Every time he came back from his long voyages—for he was trading far and near, like the greatest of merchants—he went at once to the banks of the river to see how his sweetheart fared. And always he brought some little present for her and threw it into the waves.

For twelve years he lived unmarried in Novgorod, and every year made voyages, buying and selling, and always growing richer and richer. Many were the mothers in Novgorod who would have liked to see him married to their daughters. Many were the pillows that were wet with the tears of the young girls, as they thought of the blue eyes of Sadko and his golden hair.

And then, in the twelfth year since he walked into Novgorod with the coffer on his shoulder, he was sailing in a ship on the Caspian Sea, far, far away. For many days the ship sailed on, and Sadko sat on deck and played his dulcimer and sang of Novgorod and of the little river Volkhov that flows under the walls of the town. Blue was the Caspian Sea, and the waves were like furrows in a field, long lines of white under the steady wind, while the sails swelled and the ship shot over the water.

And suddenly the ship stopped.

In the middle of the sea, far from land, the ship stopped and trembled in the waves, as if she were held by a big hand.

"We are aground!" cry the sailors; and the captain, the great one, tells them to take soundings. Seventy fathoms by the bow it was, and seventy fathoms by the stern.

"We are not aground," says the captain, "unless there is a rock sticking up like a needle in the middle of the Caspian Sea!"

"There is magic in this," say the sailors.

"Hoist more sail," says the captain; and up go the white sails, selling out in the wind, while the masts bend and creak. But still the ship lay shivering and did not move, out there in the middle of the sea.

"Hoist more sail yet," says the captain; and up go the white sails, swelling and tugging, while the masts creak and groan. But still the ship lay there shivering and did not move.

"There is an unlucky one aboard," says an old sailor. "We must draw lots and find him, and throw him overboard into the sea."

The other sailors agreed to this. And still Sadko sat, and played his dulcimer and sang.

The sailors cut pieces of string, all of a length, as many as there were souls in the ship, and one of those strings they cut in half. Then they made them into a bundle, and each man plucked one string. And Sadko stopped his playing for a moment to pluck a string, and his was the string that had been cut in half.

"Magician, sorcerer, unclean one!" shouted the sailors.

"Not so," said Sadko. "I remember now an old promise I made, and I keep it willingly."

He took his dulcimer in his hand, and leapt from the ship into the blue Caspian Sea. The waves had scarcely closed over his head before the ship shot forward again, and flew over the waves like a swan's feather, and came in the end safely to her harbour.

Sadko dropped into the waves, and the waves closed over him. Down he sank, like a pebble thrown into a pool, down and down. First the water was blue, then green, and strange fish with goggle eyes and golden fins swam round him as he sank. He came at last to the bottom of the sea.

And there, on the bottom of the sea, was a palace built of green wood. Yes, all the timbers of all the ships that have been wrecked in all the seas of the world are in that palace, and they are all green, and cunningly fitted together, so that the palace is worth a ten days' journey only to see it. And in front of the palace Sadko saw two big kobbly sturgeons, each a hundred and fifty feet long, lashing their tails and guarding the gates. Now, sturgeons are the oldest of all fish, and these were the oldest of all sturgeons.

Sadko walked between the sturgeons and through the gates of the palace. Inside there was a great hall, and the Tzar of the Sea lay resting in the hall, with his gold crown on his head and his blue hair floating round him in the water, and his great body covered with scales lying along the hall. The Tzar of the Sea filled the hall—and there is room in that hall for a village. And there were fish swimming this way and that in and out of the windows.

"Ah, Sadko," says the Tzar of the Sea, "you took what the sea gave you, but you have been a long time in coming to sing in the palaces of the sea. Twelve years I have lain here waiting for you."

"Great Tzar, forgive," says Sadko.

"Sing now," says the Tzar of the Sea, and his voice was like the beating of waves.

And Sadko played on his dulcimer and sang.

He sang of Novgorod and of the little river Volkhov which he loved. It was in his song that none of the girls of Novgorod were as pretty as the little river. And there was the sound of wind over the lake in his song, the sound of ripples under the prow of a boat, the sound of ripples on the shore, the sound of the river flowing past the tall reeds, the whispering sound of the river at night. And all the time he played cunningly on the dulcimer. The girls of Novgorod had never danced to so sweet a tune when in the old days Sadko played his dulcimer to earn kopecks and crusts of bread.

Never had the Tzar of the Sea heard such music.

"I would dance," said the Tzar of the Sea, and he stood up like a tall tree in the hall.

"Play on," said the Tzar of the Sea, and he strode through the gates. The sturgeons guarding the gates stirred the water with their tails.

And if the Tzar of the Sea was huge in the hall, he was huger still when he stood outside on the bottom of the sea. He grew taller and taller, towering like a mountain. His feet were like small hills. His blue hair hung down to his waist, and he was covered with green scales. And he began to dance on the bottom of the sea.

Great was that dancing. The sea boiled, and ships went down. The waves rolled as big as houses. The sea overflowed its shores, and whole towns were under water as the Tzar danced mightily on the bottom of the sea. Hither and thither rushed the waves, and the very earth shook at the dancing of that tremendous Tzar.

He danced till he was tired, and then he came back to the palace of green wood, and passed the sturgeons, and shrank into himself and came through the gates into the hall, where Sadko still played on his dulcimer and sang.

"You have played well and given me pleasure," says the Tzar of the Sea. "I have thirty daughters, and you shall choose one and marry her, and be a Prince of the Sea."

He began to dance on the bottom of the sea.

"Better than all maidens I love my little river," says Sadko; and the Tzar of the Sea laughed and threw his head back, with his blue hair floating all over the hall.

And then there came in the thirty daughters of the Tzar of the Sea. Beautiful they were, lovely, and graceful; but twenty-nine of them passed by, and Sadko fingered his dulcimer and thought of his little river.

There came in the thirtieth, and Sadko cried out aloud. "Here is the only maiden in the world as pretty as my little river!" says he. And she looked at him with eyes that shone like stars reflected in the river. Her hair was dark, like the river at night. She laughed, and her voice was like the flowing of the river.

"And what is the name of your little river?" says the Tzar.

"It is the little river Volkhov that flows by Novgorod," says Sadko; "but your daughter is as fair as the little river, and I would gladly marry her if she will have me."

"It is a strange thing," says the Tzar, "but Volkhov is the name of my youngest daughter."

He put Sadko's hand in the hand of his youngest daughter, and they kissed each other. And as they kissed, Sadko saw a necklace round her neck, and knew it for one he had thrown into the river as a present for his sweetheart.

She smiled, and "Come!" says she, and took him away to a palace of her own, and showed him a coffer; and in that coffer were bracelets and rings and earrings—all the gifts that he had thrown into the river.

And Sadko laughed for joy, and kissed the youngest daughter of the Tzar of the Sea, and she kissed him back.

"O my little river!" says he; "there is no girl in all the world but thou as pretty as my little river."

Well, they were married, and the Tzar of the Sea laughed at the wedding feast till the palace shook and the fish swam off in all directions.

And after the feast Sadko and his bride went off together to her palace. And before they slept she kissed him very tenderly, and she said,—

"O Sadko, you will not forget me? You will play to me sometimes, and sing?"

"I shall never lose sight of you, my pretty one," says he; "and as for music, I will sing and play all the day long."

"That's as may be," says she, and they fell asleep.

And in the middle of the night Sadko happened to turn in bed, and he touched the Princess with his left foot, and she was cold, cold, cold as ice in January. And with that touch of cold he woke, and he was lying under the walls of Novgorod, with his dulcimer in his hand, and one of his feet was in the little river Volkhov, and the moon was shining.

After that some say he went into the town, and lived on alone until he died. Others say that he took his dulcimer and swam out into the middle of the river, and sank under water again, looking for his little Princess. They say he found her, and lives still in the green palaces of the bottom of the sea; and when there is a big storm, you may know that Sadko is playing on his dulcimer and singing, and that the Tzar of the Sea is dancing his tremendous dance down there, on the bottom, under the waves.

Frost

ONCE UPON a time there were an old man and an old woman. Now the old woman was the old man's second wife. His first wife had died, and had left him with a little daughter: Martha she was called. Then he married again, and God gave him a cross wife, and with her two more daughters, and they were very different from the first.

The old woman loved her own daughters, and gave them red kisel jelly every day, and honey too, as much as they could put into their greedy little mouths. But poor little Martha, the eldest, she got only what the others left. When they were cross they threw away what they left, and then she got nothing at all.

The children grew older, and the stepmother made Martha do all the work of the house. She had to fetch the wood for the stove, and light it and keep it burning. She had to draw the water for her sisters to wash their hands in. She had to make the clothes, and wash them and mend them. She had to cook the dinner, and clean the dishes after the others had done before having a bite for herself.

For all that the stepmother was never satisfied, and was for ever shouting at her: "Look, the kettle is in the wrong place;" "There is dust on the floor;" "There is a spot on the tablecloth;" or, "The spoons are not clean,

13

you stupid, ugly, idle hussy." But Martha was not idle. She worked all day long, and got up before the sun, while her sisters never stirred from their beds till it was time for dinner. And she was not stupid. She always had a song on her lips, except when her stepmother had beaten her. And as for being ugly, she was the prettiest little girl in the village.

Her father saw all this, but he could not do anything, for the old woman was mistress at home, and he was terribly afraid of her. And as for the daughters, they saw how their mother treated Martha, and they did the same. They were always complaining and getting her into trouble. It was a pleasure to them to see the tears on her pretty cheeks.

Well, time went on, and the little girl grew up, and the daughters of the stepmother were as ugly as could be. Their eyes were always cross, and their mouths were always complaining. Their mother saw that no one would want to marry either of them while there was Martha about the house, with her bright eyes and her songs and her kindness to everybody.

So she thought of a way to get rid of her stepdaughter, and a cruel way it was.

"See here, old man," says she, "it is high time Martha was married, and I have a bridegroom in mind for her. To-morrow morning you must harness the old mare to the sledge, and put a bit of food together and be ready to start early, as I'd like to see you back before night."

To Martha she said: "To-morrow you must pack your things in a box, and put on your best dress to show yourself to your betrothed."

"Who is he?" asked Martha with red cheeks.

"You will know when you see him," said the step-mother.

All that night Martha hardly slept. She could hardly believe that she was really going to escape from the old woman at last, and have a hut of her own, where there would be no one to scold her. She wondered who the young man was. She hoped he was Fedor Ivanovitch, who had such kind eyes, and such nimble fingers on the balalaika, and such a merry way of flinging out his heels when he danced the Russian dance. But although he always smiled at her when they met, she felt she hardly dared to hope that it was he. Early in the morning she got up and said her prayers to God, put the whole hut in order, and packed her things into a little box. That was easy, because she had such few things. It was the other daughters who had new dresses. Any old thing was good enough for Martha. But she put on her best blue dress, and there she was, as pretty a little maid as ever walked under the birch trees in spring.

The old man harnessed the mare to the sledge and brought it to the door. The snow was very deep and frozen hard, and the wind peeled the skin from his ears before he covered them with the flaps of his fur hat.

"Sit down at the table and have a bite before you go," says the old woman.

The old man sat down, and his daughter with him, and drank a glass of tea and ate some black bread. And the old woman put some cabbage soup, left from the day before, in a saucer, and said to Martha, "Eat this, my little pigeon, and get ready for the road." But when she said "my little pigeon," she did not smile with her eyes, but only with her cruel mouth, and Martha was afraid. The old woman whispered to the old man: "I have a word for you, old fellow. You will take Martha to her betrothed, and I'll tell you the way. You go straight along, and then take the road to the right into the forest . . . you know . . . straight to the big fir tree that stands on a hillock, and there you will give Martha to her betrothed and leave her. He will be waiting for her, and his name is Frost."

The old man stared, opened his mouth, and stopped eating. The little maid, who had heard the last words, began to cry.

"Now, what are you whimpering about?" screamed the old woman. "Frost is a rich bridegroom and a handsome one. See how much he owns. All the pines and firs are his, and the birch trees. Any one would envy his possessions, and he himself is a very bogatir,* a man of strength and power."

The old man trembled, and said nothing in reply. And Martha went on crying quietly, though she tried to stop her tears. The old man packed up what was left of the black bread, told Martha to put on her sheepskin coat, set her in the sledge and climbed in, and drove off along the white, frozen road.

The road was long and the country open, and the wind grew colder and colder, while the frozen snow blew up from under the hoofs of the mare and spattered the sledge with white patches. The tale is soon told, but it takes time to happen, and the sledge was white all over long before they turned off into the forest.

They came in the end deep into the forest, and left

---

*The bogatirs were strong men, heroes of old Russia.

the road, and over the deep snow through the trees to the great fir. There the old man stopped, told his daughter to get out of the sledge, set her little box under the fir, and said, "Wait here for your bridegroom, and when he comes be sure to receive him with kind words." Then he turned the mare round and drove home, with the tears running from his eyes and freezing on his cheeks before they had had time to reach his beard.

The little maid sat and trembled. Her sheepskin coat was worn through, and in her blue bridal dress she sat, while fits of shivering shook her whole body. She wanted to run away; but she had not strength to move, or even to keep her little white teeth from chattering between her frozen lips.

Suddenly, not far away, she heard Frost crackling among the fir trees. He was leaping from tree to tree, crackling as he came.

He leapt at last into the great fir tree, under which the little maid was sitting. He crackled in the top of the tree, and then called down out of the topmost branches,—

"Are you warm, little maid?"

"Warm, warm, little Father Frost."

Frost laughed, and came a little lower in the tree and crackled and crackled louder than before. Then he asked,—

"Are you still warm, little maid? Are you warm, little red cheeks?"

The little maid could hardly speak. She was nearly dead, but she answered,—

"Warm, dear Frost; warm, little father."

Frost climbed lower in the tree, and crackled louder than ever, and asked,—

"Are you still warm, little maid? Are you warm, little red cheeks? Are you warm, little paws?"

The little maid was benumbed all over, but she whispered so that Frost could just hear her,—

"Warm, little pigeon, warm, dear Frost."

And Frost was sorry for her, leapt down with a tremendous crackle and a scattering of frozen snow, wrapped the little maid up in rich furs, and covered her with warm blankets.

In the morning the old woman said to her husband, "Drive off now to the forest, and wake the young couple."

The old man wept when he thought of his little daughter, for he was sure that he would find her dead. He harnessed the mare, and drove off through the snow. He came to the tree, and heard his little daughter singing merrily, while Frost crackled and laughed. There she was, alive and warm, with a good fur cloak about her shoulders, a rich veil, costly blankets round her feet, and a box full of splendid presents.

The old man did not say a word. He was too surprised. He just sat in the sledge staring, while the little maid lifted her box and the box of presents, set them in the sledge, climbed in, and sat down beside him.

They came home, and the little maid, Martha, fell at the feet of her stepmother. The old woman nearly went off her head with rage when she saw her alive, with her fur cloak and rich veil, and the box of splendid presents fit for the daughter of a prince.

"Ah, you chit," she cried, "you won't get round me like that!"

And she would not say another word to the little

There she was, alive and warm,
with a good fur cloak about her shoulders.

maid, but went about all day long biting her nails and thinking what to do.

At night she said to the old man,—

"You must take my daughters, too, to that bride-groom in the forest. He will give them better gifts than these."

Things take time to happen, but the tale is quickly told. Early next morning the old woman woke her daughters, fed them with good food, dressed them like brides, hustled the old man, made him put clean hay in the sledge and warm blankets, and sent them off to the forest.

The old man did as he was bid—drove to the big fir tree, set the boxes under the tree, lifted out the step-daughters and set them on the boxes side by side, and drove back home.

They were warmly dressed, these two, and well fed, and at first, as they sat there, they did not think about the cold.

"I can't think what put it into mother's head to marry us both at once," said the first, "and to send us here to be married. As if there were not enough young men in the village. Who can tell what sort of fellows we shall meet here!"

Then they began to quarrel.

"Well," says one of them, "I'm beginning to get the cold shivers. If our fated ones do not come soon, we shall perish of cold."

"It's a flat lie to say that bridegrooms get ready early. It's already dinner-time."

"What if only one comes?"

"You'll have to come another time."

"You think he'll look at you?"

"Well, he won't take you, anyhow."

"Of course he'll take me."

"Take you first! It's enough to make any one laugh!"

They began to fight and scratch each other, so that their cloaks fell open and the cold entered their bosoms.

Frost, crackling among the trees, laughing to himself, froze the hands of the two quarrelling girls, and they hid their hands in the sleeves of their fur coats and shivered, and went on scolding and jeering at each other.

"Oh, you ugly mug, dirty nose! What sort of a house-keeper will you make?"

"And what about you, boasting one? You know nothing but how to gad about and lick your own face. We'll soon see which of us he'll take."

And the two girls went on wrangling and wrangling till they began to freeze in good earnest.

Suddenly they cried out together,—

"Devil take these bridegrooms for being so long in coming! You have turned blue all over."

And together they replied, shivering,—

"No bluer than yourself, tooth-chatterer."

And Frost, not so far away, crackled and laughed, and leapt from fir tree to fir tree, crackling as he came.

The girls heard that some one was coming through the forest.

"Listen! there's some one coming. Yes, and with bells on his sledge!"

"Shut up, you chit! I can't hear, and the frost is taking the skin off me."

They began blowing on their fingers.

And Frost came nearer and nearer, crackling, laughing, talking to himself. Nearer and nearer he came, leaping from tree-top to tree-top, till at last he leapt into the great fir under which the two girls were sitting and quarrelling.

He leant down, looking through the branches, and asked,—

"Are you warm, maidens? Are you warm, little red cheeks? Are you warm, little pigeons?"

"Ugh, Frost, the cold is hurting us. We are frozen. We are waiting for our bridegrooms, but the cursed fellows have not turned up."

Frost came a little lower in the tree, and crackled louder and swifter.

"Are you warm, maidens? Are you warm, my little red cheeks?"

"Go to the devil!" they cried out. "Are you blind? Our hands and feet are frozen!"

Frost came still lower in the branches, and cracked and crackled louder than ever.

"Are you warm, maidens?" he asked.

"Into the pit with you, with all the fiends," the girls screamed at him, "you ugly, wretched fellow!" . . . And as they were cursing at him their bad words died on their lips, for the two girls, the cross children of the cruel stepmother, were frozen stiff where they sat.

Frost hung from the lowest branches of the tree, swaying and crackling while he looked at the anger frozen on their faces. Then he climbed swiftly up again, and crackling and cracking, chuckling to himself, he went off, leaping from fir tree to fir tree, this way and that through the white, frozen forest.

In the morning the old woman says to her husband,—

"Now then, old man, harness the mare to the sledge, and put new hay in the sledge to be warm for my little ones, and lay fresh rushes on the hay to be soft for them; and take warm rugs with you, for maybe they will be cold, even in their furs. And look sharp about it, and don't keep them waiting. The frost is hard this morning, and it was harder in the night."

The old man had not time to eat even a mouthful of black bread before she had driven him out into the snow. He put hay and rushes and soft blankets in the sledge, and harnessed the mare, and went off to the forest. He came to the great fir, and found the two girls sitting under it dead, with their anger still to be seen on their frozen, ugly faces.

He picked them up, first one and then the other, and put them in the rushes and the warm hay, covered them with the blankets, and drove home.

The old woman saw him coming, far away, over the shining snow. She ran to meet him, and shouted out,—

"Where are the little ones?"

"In the sledge."

She snatched off the blankets and pulled aside the rushes, and found the bodies of her two cross daughters.

Instantly she flew at the old man in a storm of rage. "What have you done to my children, my little red cherries, my little pigeons? I will kill you with the oven fork! I will break your head with the poker!"

The old man listened till she was out of breath and could not say another word. That is the only wise thing to do when somebody is in a scolding rage. And as soon as she had no breath left with which to answer him, he said,—

"My little daughter got riches for soft words, but yours were always rough of the tongue. And it's not my fault, anyhow, for you yourself sent them into the forest."

Well, at last the old woman got her breath again, and scolded away till she was tired out. But in the end she made her peace with the old man, and they lived together as quietly as could be expected.

As for Martha, Fedor Ivanovitch sought her in marriage, as he had meant to do all along—yes, and married her; and pretty she looked in the furs that Frost had given her. And she had the prettiest children that ever were seen—yes, and the best behaved. For if ever they thought of being naughty, the old grandfather told them the story of crackling Frost, and how kind words won kindness, and cross words cold treatment.

The Three Men of Power

L ONG AGO there lived a King, and he had three
daughters, the loveliest in all the world. He loved
them so well that he built a palace for them underground, lest the rough winds should blow on them or
the red sun scorch their delicate faces. A wonderful
palace it was, down there underground, with fountains
and courts, and lamps burning, and precious stones
glittering in the light of the lamps. And the three lovely
princesses grew up in that palace underground, and
knew no other light but that of the coloured lanterns,
and had never seen the broad world that lies open
under the sun by day and under the stars by night.
Indeed, they did not know that there was a world outside those glittering walls, above that shining ceiling,
carved and gilded and set with precious stones.

But it so happened that among the books that were
given them to read was one in which was written of the
world: how the sun shines in the sky; how trees grow
green; how the grass waves in the wind and the leaves
whisper together; how the rivers flow between their
green banks and through the flowery meadows, until
they come to the blue sea that joins the earth and the
sky. They read in that book of white-walled towns, of
churches with gilded and painted domes, of the brown
wooden huts of the peasants, of the great forests, of the

ships on the rivers, and of the long roads with the folk moving on them, this way and that, about the world.

And when the King came to see them, as he was used to do, they asked him,—

"Father, is it true that there is a garden in the world?"

"Yes," said the King.

"And green grass?"

"Yes," said the King.

"And little shining flowers?"

"Why, yes," said the King, wondering and stroking his silver beard.

And the three lovely princesses all begged him at once,—

"Oh, your Majesty, our own little father, whom we love, let us out to see this world. Let us out just so that we may see this garden, and walk in it on the green grass, and see the shining flowers."

The King turned his head away and tried not to listen to them. But what could he do? They were the loveliest princesses in the world, and when they begged him just to let them walk in the garden he could see the tears in their eyes. And after all, he thought, there were high walls to the garden.

So he called up his army, and set soldiers all round the garden, and a hundred soldiers to each gate, so that no one should come in. And then he let the princesses come up from their underground palace, and step out into the sunshine in the garden, with ten nurses and maids to each princess to see that no harm came to her.

The princesses stepped out into the garden, under the blue sky, shading their eyes at first because they had never before been in the golden sunlight. Soon they were taking hands, and running this way and that along the garden paths and over the green grass, and gathering posies of shining flowers to set in their girdles and to shame their golden crowns. And the King sat and watched them with love in his eyes, and was glad to see how happy they were. And after all, he thought, what with the high walls and the soldiers standing to arms, nothing could get in to hurt them.

But just as he had quieted his old heart a strong whirlwind came down out of the blue sky, tearing up trees and throwing them aside, and lifting the roofs from the houses. But it did not touch the palace roofs, shining green in the sunlight, and it plucked no trees from the garden. It raged this way and that, and then with its swift whirling arms it caught up the three lovely princesses, and carried them up into the air, over the high walls and over the heads of the guarding soldiers. For a moment the King saw them, his daughters, the three lovely princesses, spinning round and round, as if they were dancing in the sky. A moment later they were no more than little whirling specks, like dust in the sunlight. And then they were out of sight, and the King and all the maids and nurses were alone in the empty garden. The noise of the wind had gone. The soldiers did not dare to speak. The only sound in the King's ears was the sobbing and weeping of the maids and nurses.

The King called his generals, and made them send the soldiers in all directions over the country to bring back the princesses, if the whirlwind should tire and set them again upon the ground. The soldiers went to the very boundaries of the kingdom, but they came back as they went. Not one of them had seen the three lovely princesses.

Then the King called together all his faithful servants, and promised a great reward to any one who should bring news of the three princesses. It was the same with the servants as with the soldiers. Far and wide they galloped out. Slowly, one by one, they rode back, with bent heads, on tired horses. Not one of them had seen the King's daughters.

Then the King called a grand council of his wise boyars and men of state. They all sat round and listened as the King told his tale and asked if one of them would not undertake the task of finding and rescuing the three princesses. "The wind has not set them down within the boundaries of my kingdom; and now, God knows, they may be in the power of wicked men or worse." He said he would give one of the princesses in marriage to any one who could follow where the wind went and bring his daughters back; yes, and besides, he would make him the richest man in the kingdom. But the boyars and the wise men of state sat round in silence. He asked them one by one. They were all silent and afraid. For they were boyars and wise men of state, and not one of them would undertake to follow the whirlwind and rescue the three princesses.

The King wept bitter tears.

"I see," he said, "I have no friends about me in the palace. My soldiers cannot, my servants cannot, and my boyars and wise men will not, bring back my three sweet maids, whom I love better than my kingdom."

And with that he sent heralds throughout the kingdom to announce the news, and to ask if there were none among the common folk, the moujiks, the simple folk like us, who would put his hand to the work of rescuing the three lovely princesses, since not one of the boyars and wise men was willing to do it.

Now, at that time in a certain village lived a poor widow, and she had three sons, strong men, true bogatirs and men of power. All three had been born in a single night: the eldest at evening, the middle one at midnight, and the youngest just as the sky was lightening with the dawn. For this reason they were called Evening, Midnight, and Sunrise. Evening was dusky, with brown eyes and hair; Midnight was dark, with eyes and hair as black as charcoal; while Sunrise had hair golden as the sun, and eyes blue as morning sky. And all three were as strong as any of the strong men and mighty bogatirs who have shaken this land of Russia with their tread.

As soon as the King's word had been proclaimed in the village, the three brothers asked for their mother's blessing, which she gave them, kissing them on the forehead and on both cheeks. Then they made ready for the journey and rode off to the capital—Evening on his horse of dusky brown, Midnight on his black horse, and Sunrise on his horse that was as white as clouds in summer. They came to the capital, and as they rode through the streets everybody stopped to look at them, and all the pretty young women waved handkerchiefs at the windows. But the three brothers looked neither to right nor left but straight before them, and they rode to the palace of the King.

They came to the King, bowed low before him, and said,—

"May you live for many years, O King. We have come to you not for feasting but for service. Let us, O King, ride out to rescue your three princesses."

"God give you success, my good young men," says the King. "What are your names?"

"We are three brothers—Evening, Midnight, and Sunrise."

"What will you have to take with you on the road?"

"For ourselves, O King, we want nothing. Only, do not leave our mother in poverty, for she is old."

The King sent for the old woman, their mother, and gave her a home in his palace, and made her eat and drink at his table, and gave her new boots made by his own cobblers, and new clothes sewn by the very sempstresses who were used to make dresses for the three daughters of the King, who were the loveliest princesses in the world, and had been carried away by the whirlwind. No old woman in Russia was better looked after than the mother of the three young bogatirs and men of power, Evening, Midnight, and Sunrise, while they were away on their adventure seeking the King's daughters.

The young men rode out on their journey. A month they rode together, two months, and in the third month they came to a broad desert plain, where there were no towns, no villages, no farms, and not a human being to be seen. They rode on over the sand, through the rank grass, over the stony wastes. At last, on the other side of that desolate plain, they came to a thick forest. They found a path through the thick undergrowth, and rode along that path together into the very heart of the forest. And there, alone in the heart of the forest, they came to a hut, with a railed yard and a shed full of cattle and sheep. They called out with their strong young voices, and were answered by the lowing of the cattle, the bleating of the sheep, and the strong wind in the tops of the great trees.

They rode through the railed yard and came to the hut. Evening leant from his brown horse and knocked on the window. There was no answer. They forced open the door, and found no one at all.

"Well, brothers," says Evening, "let us make ourselves at home. Let us stay here awhile. We have been riding three months. Let us rest, and then ride farther. We shall deal better with our adventure if we come to it as fresh men, and not dusty and weary from the long road."

The others agreed. They tied up their horses, fed them, drew water from the well, and gave them to drink; and then, tired out, they went into the hut, said their prayers to God, and lay down to sleep with their weapons close to their hands, like true bogatirs and men of power.

In the morning the youngest brother, Sunrise, said to the eldest brother, Evening,—

"Midnight and I are going hunting to-day, and you shall rest here, and see what sort of dinner you can give us when we come back."

"Very well," says Evening; "but to-morrow I shall go hunting, and one of you shall stay here and cook the dinner."

Nobody made bones about that, and so Evening

stood at the door of the hut while the others rode off—
Midnight on his black horse, and Sunrise on his horse,
white as a summer cloud. They rode off into the forest,
and disappeared among the green trees.

Evening watched them out of sight, and then, without thinking twice about what he was doing, went out
into the yard, picked out the finest sheep he could see,
caught it, killed it, skinned it, cleaned it, and set it in a
cauldron on the stove so as to be ready and hot whenever his brothers should come riding back from the forest. As soon as that was done, Evening lay down on the
broad bench to rest himself.

He had scarcely lain down before there were a knocking and a rattling and a stumbling, and the door
opened, and in walked a little man a yard high, with a
beard seven yards long flowing out behind him over
both his shoulders. He looked round angrily, and saw
Evening, who yawned, and sat up on the bench, and
began chuckling at the sight of him. The little man
screamed out,—

"What are you chuckling about? How dare you play
the master in my house? How dare you kill my best
sheep?"

Evening answered him, laughing,—

"Grow a little bigger, and it won't be so hard to see
you down there. Till then it will be better for you to
keep a civil tongue in your head."

The little man was angry before, but now he was
angrier.

"What?" he screamed. "I am little, am I? Well, see
what little does!"

And with that he grabbed an old crust of bread, leapt

on Evening's shoulders, and began beating him over the head. Yes, and the little fellow was so strong he beat Evening till he was half dead, and was blind in one eye and could not see out of the other. Then, when he was tired, he threw Evening under the bench, took the sheep out of the cauldron, gobbled it up in a few mouthfuls, and, when he had done, went off again into the forest.

When Evening came to his senses again, he bound up his head with a dishcloth, and lay on the ground and groaned.

Midnight and Sunrise rode back, on the black horse and the white, and came to the hut, where they found their brother groaning on the ground, unable to see out of his eyes, and with a dishcloth round his head.

"What are you tied up like that for?" they asked; "and where is our dinner?"

Evening was ashamed to tell them the truth—how he had been thumped about with a crust of bread by a little fellow only a yard high. He moaned and said,—

"O my brothers, I made a fire in the stove, and fell ill from the great heat in this little hut. My head ached. All day I lay senseless, and could neither boil nor roast. I thought my head would burst with the heat, and my brains fly beyond the seventh world."

Next day Sunrise went hunting with Evening, whose head was still bound up in a dishcloth, and hurting so sorely that he could hardly see. Midnight stayed at home. It was his turn to see to the dinner. Sunrise rode out on his cloud-white horse, and Evening on his dusky brown. Midnight stood in the doorway of the hut, watched them disappear among the green trees, and then set about getting the dinner.

He lit the fire, but was careful not to make it too hot. Then he went into the yard, caught the very fattest of the sheep, killed it, skinned it, cleaned it, cut it up, and set it on the stove. Then, when all was ready, he lay down on the bench and rested himself.

But before he had lain there long there were a knocking, a stamping, a rattling, a grumbling, and in came the little old man, one yard high, with a beard seven yards long, and without wasting words the little fellow leapt on the shoulders of the bogatir, and set to beating him and thumping him, first on one side of his head and then on the other. He gave him such a banging that he very nearly made an end of him altogether. Then the little fellow ate up the whole of the sheep in a few mouthfuls, and went off angrily into the forest, with his long white beard flowing behind him.

Midnight tied up his head with a handkerchief, and lay down under the bench, groaning and groaning, unable to put his head to the ground, or even to lay it in the crook of his arm, it was so bruised by the beating given it by the little old man.

In the evening the brothers rode back, and found Midnight groaning under the bench, with his head bound up in a handkerchief.

Evening looked at him and said nothing. Perhaps he was thinking of his own bruised head, which was still tied up in a dishcloth.

"What's the matter with you?" says Sunrise.

"There never was such another stove as this," says Midnight. "I'd no sooner lit it than it seemed as if the whole hut were on fire. My head nearly burst. It's aching now; and as for your dinner, why, I've not been able to put a hand to anything all day."

Evening chuckled to himself, but Sunrise only said, "That's bad, brother; but you shall go hunting tomorrow, and I'll stay at home, and see what I can do with the stove."

And so on the third day the two elder brothers went hunting—Midnight on his black horse, and Evening on his horse of dusky brown. Sunrise stood in the doorway of the hut, and saw them disappear under the green trees. The sun shone on his golden curls, and his blue eyes were like the sky itself. There never was such another bogatir as he.

He went into the hut and lit the stove. Then he went out into the yard, chose the best sheep he could find, killed it, skinned it, cleaned it, cut it up, and set it on the stove. He made everything ready, and then lay down on the bench.

Before he had lain there very long he heard a stumping, a thumping, a knocking, a rattling, a grumbling, a rumbling. Sunrise leaped up from the bench and looked out through the window of the hut. There in the yard was the little old man, one yard high, with a beard seven yards long. He was carrying a whole haystack on his head and a great tub of water in his arms. He came into the middle of the yard, and set down his tub to water all the beasts. He set down the haystack and scattered the hay about. All the cattle and the sheep came together to eat and to drink, and the little man stood and counted them. He counted the oxen, he counted the goats, and then he counted the sheep. He counted them once, and his eyes began to flash. He counted them twice, and he began to grind his teeth. He counted them a third time, made sure that one was missing, and then he flew into a violent rage, rushed across the yard and into the hut, and gave Sunrise a terrific blow on the head.

Sunrise shook his head as if a fly had settled on it. Then he jumped suddenly and caught the end of the long beard of the little old man, and set to pulling him this way and that, round and round the hut, as if his beard was a rope. Phew! how the little man roared.

Sunrise laughed, and tugged him this way and that, and mocked him, crying out, "If you do not know the ford, it is better not to go into the water," meaning that the little fellow had begun to beat him without finding out who was the stronger.

The little old man, one yard high, with a beard seven yards long, began to pray and to beg,—

"O man of power, O great and mighty bogatir, have mercy upon me. Do not kill me. Leave me my soul to repent with."

Sunrise laughed, and dragged the little fellow out into the yard, whirled him round at the end of his beard, and brought him to a great oak trunk that lay on the ground. Then with a heavy iron wedge he fixed the end of the little man's beard firmly in the oaken trunk, and, leaving the little man howling and lamenting, went back to the hut, set it in order again, saw that the sheep was cooking as it should, and then lay down in peace to wait for the coming of his brothers.

Evening and Midnight rode home, leapt from their horses, and came into the hut to see how the little man had dealt with their brother. They could hardly believe their eyes when they saw him alive and well, without a bruise, lying comfortably on the bench.

He sat up and laughed in their faces.

"Well, brothers," says he, "come along with me into the yard, and I think I can show you that headache of yours. It's a good deal stronger than it is big, but for the time being you need not be afraid of it, for it's fastened to an oak timber that all three of us together could not lift."

He got up and went into the yard. Evening and Midnight followed him with shamed faces. But when they came to the oaken timber the little man was not there. Long ago he had torn himself free and run away into the forest. But half his beard was left, wedged in the trunk, and Sunrise pointed to that and said,—

"Tell me, brothers, was it the heat of the stove that gave you your headaches? Or had this long beard something to do with it?"

The brothers grew red, and laughed, and told him the whole truth.

Meanwhile Sunrise had been looking at the end of the beard, the end of the half beard that was left, and he saw that it had been torn out by the roots, and that drops of blood from the little man's chin showed the way he had gone.

Quickly the brothers went back to the hut and ate up the sheep. Then they leapt on their horses, and rode off into the green forest, following the drops of blood that had fallen from the little man's chin. For three days they rode through the green forest, until at last the red drops of the trail led them to a deep pit, a black hole in the earth, hidden by thick bushes and going far down into the underworld.

Sunrise left his brothers to guard the hole, while he went off into the forest and gathered bast, and twisted it, and made a strong rope, and brought it to the mouth of the pit, and asked his brothers to lower him down.

He made a loop in the rope. His brothers kissed him on both cheeks, and he kissed them back. Then he sat in the loop, the Evening and Midnight lowered him down into the darkness. Down and down he went, swinging in the dark, till he came into a world under the world, with a light that was neither that of the sun, nor of the moon, nor of the stars. He stepped from the loop in the rope of twisted bast, and set out walking through the underworld, going whither his eyes led him, for he found no more drops of blood, nor any other traces of the little old man.

He walked and walked, and came at last to a palace of copper, green and ruddy in the strange light. He went into that palace, and there came to meet him in the copper halls a maiden whose cheeks were redder than the aloe and whiter than the snow. She was the youngest daughter of the King, and the loveliest of the three princesses, who were the loveliest in all the world. Sweetly she curtsied to Sunrise, as he stood there with his golden hair and his eyes blue as the sky at morning, and sweetly she asked him,—

"How have you come hither, my brave young man— of your own will or against it?"

"Your father has sent to rescue you and your sisters."

She bade him sit at the table, and gave him food and brought him a little flask of the water of strength.

"Strong you are," says she, "but not strong enough for what is before you. Drink this, and your strength will be greater than it is; for you will need all the strength you have and can win, if you are to rescue us and live."

Sunrise looked in her sweet eyes, and drank the water of strength in a single draught, and felt gigantic power forcing its way throughout his body.

"Now," thought he, "let come what may."

Instantly a violent wind rushed through the copper palace, and the Princess trembled.

"The snake that holds me here is coming," says she. "He is flying hither on his strong wings."

She took the great hand of the bogatir in her little fingers, and drew him to another room, and hid him there.

The copper palace rocked in the wind, and there flew into the great hall a huge snake with three heads. The snake hissed loudly, and called out in a whistling voice,—

"I smell the smell of a Russian soul. What visitor have you here?"

"How could any one come here?" said the Princess. "You have been flying over Russia. There you smelt Russian souls, and the smell is still in your nostrils, so that you think you smell them here."

"It is true," said the snake: "I have been flying over Russia. I have flown far. Let me eat and drink, for I am both hungry and thirsty."

All this time Sunrise was watching from the other room.

The Princess brought meat and drink to the snake, and in the drink she put a philtre of sleep.

The snake ate and drank, and began to feel sleepy. He

coiled himself up in rings, laid his three heads in the lap of the Princess, told her to scratch them for him, and dropped into a deep sleep.

The Princess called Sunrise, and the bogatir rushed in, swung his glittering sword three times round his golden head, and cut off all three heads of the snake. It was like felling three oak trees at a single blow. Then he made a great fire of wood, and threw upon it the body of the snake, and, when it was burnt up, scattered the ashes over the open country.

"And now fare you well," says Sunrise to the Princess; but she threw her arms about his neck.

"Fare you well," says he. "I go to seek your sisters. As soon as I have found them I will come back."

And at that she let him go.

He walked on further through the underworld, and came at last to a palace of silver, gleaming in the strange light.

He went in there, and was met with sweet words and kindness by the second of the three lovely princesses. In that palace he killed a snake with six heads. The Princess begged him to stay; but he told her he had yet to find her eldest sister. At that she wished him the help of God, and he left her, and went on further.

He walked and walked, and came at last to a palace of gold, glittering in the light of the underworld. All happened as in the other palaces. The eldest of the three daughters of the King met him with courtesy and kindness. And he killed a snake with twelve heads and freed the Princess from her imprisonment. The Princess rejoiced, and thanked Sunrise, and set about her packing to go home.

And this was the way of her packing. She went out into the broad courtyard and waved a scarlet handkerchief, and instantly the whole palace, golden and glittering, and the kingdom belonging to it, became little, little, little, till it went into a little golden egg. The Princess tied the egg in a corner of her handkerchief, and set out with Sunrise to join her sisters and go home to her father.

Her sisters did their packing in the same way. The silver palace and its kingdom were packed by the second sister into a little silver egg. And when they came to the copper palace, the youngest of the three lovely princesses clapped her hands and kissed Sunrise on both his cheeks, and waved a scarlet handkerchief, and instantly the copper palace and its kingdom were packed into a little copper egg, shining ruddy and green.

And so Sunrise and the three daughters of the King came to the foot of the deep hole down which he had come into the underworld. And there was the rope hanging with the loop at its end. And they sat in the loop, and Evening and Midnight pulled them up one by one, rejoicing together. Then the three brothers took, each of them, a princess with him on his horse, and they all rode together back to the old King, telling tales and singing songs as they went. The Princess from the golden palace rode with Evening on his horse of dusky brown; the Princess from the silver palace rode with Midnight on his horse as black as charcoal; but the Princess from the copper palace, the youngest of them all, rode with Sunrise on his horse, white as a summer cloud. Merry was the journey through the green forest, and gladly they rode over the open plain, till they came at last to the palace of her father.

There was the old King, sitting melancholy alone, when the three brothers with the princesses rode into the courtyard of the palace. The old King was so glad that he laughed and cried at the same time, and his tears ran down his beard.

"Ah me!" says the old King, "I am old, and you young men have brought my daughters back from the very world under the world. Safer they will be if they have you to guard them, even than they were in the palace I had built for them underground. But I have only one kingdom and three daughters."

"Do not trouble about that," laughed the three princesses, and they all rode out together into the open country, and there the princesses broke their eggs, one after the other, and there were the palaces of silver, copper, and gold, with the kingdoms belonging to them, and the cattle and the sheep and the goats. There was a kingdom for each of the brothers. Then they made a great feast, and had three weddings all together, and the old King sat with the mother of the three strong men, and men of power, the noble bogatirs, Evening, Midnight, and Sunrise, sitting at his side. Great was the feasting, loud were the songs, and the King made Sunrise his heir, so that some day he would wear his crown. But little did Sunrise think of that. He thought of nothing but the youngest Princess. And little she thought of it, for she had no eyes but for Sunrise. And merrily they lived together in the copper palace. And happily they rode together on the horse that was as white as clouds in summer.

Baba Yaga

ONCE UPON a time there was a widowed old man who lived alone in a hut with his little daughter. Very merry they were together, and they used to smile at each other over a table just piled with bread and jam. Everything went well, until the old man took it into his head to marry again.

Yes, the old man became foolish in the years of his old age, and he took another wife. And so the poor little girl had a stepmother. And after that everything changed. There was no more bread and jam on the table, and no more playing bo-peep, first this side of the samovar and then that, as she sat with her father at tea. It was worse than that, for she never did sit at tea. The stepmother said that everything that went wrong was the little girl's fault. And the old man believed his new wife, and so there were no more kind words for his little daughter. Day after day the stepmother used to say that the little girl was too naughty to sit at table. And then she would throw her a crust and tell her to get out of the hut and go and eat it somewhere else.

And the poor little girl used to go away by herself into the shed in the yard, and wet the dry crust with her tears, and eat it all alone. Ah me! she often wept for the old days, and she often wept at the thought of the days that were to come.

Mostly she wept because she was all alone, until one day she found a little friend in the shed. She was hunched up in a corner of the shed, eating her crust and crying bitterly, when she heard a little noise. It was like this: scratch—scratch. It was just that, a little gray mouse who lived in a hole.

Out he came, his little pointed nose and his long whiskers, his little round ears and his bright eyes. Out came his little humpy body and his long tail. And then he sat up on his hind legs, and curled his tail twice round himself and looked at the little girl.

The little girl, who had a kind heart, forgot all her sorrows, and took a scrap of her crust and threw it to the little mouse. The mouseykin nibbled and nibbled, and there, it was gone, and he was looking for another. She gave him another bit, and presently that was gone, and another and another, until there was no crust left for the little girl. Well, she didn't mind that. You see, she was so happy seeing the little mouse nibbling and nibbling.

When the crust was done the mouseykin looks up at her with his little bright eyes, and "Thank you," he says, in a little squeaky voice. "Thank you," he says; "you are a kind little girl, and I am only a mouse, and I've eaten all your crust. But there is one thing I can do for you, and that is to tell you to take care. The old woman in the hut (and that was the cruel stepmother) is own sister to Baba Yaga, the bony-legged, the witch. So if ever she sends you on a message to your aunt, you come and tell me. For Baba Yaga would eat you soon enough with her iron teeth if you did not know what to do."

"Oh, thank you," said the little girl; and just then she heard the stepmother calling to her to come in and clean up the tea things, and tidy the house, and brush out the floor, and clean everybody's boots.

So off she had to go.

When she went in she had a good look at her stepmother, and sure enough she had a long nose, and she was as bony as a fish with all the flesh picked off, and the little girl thought of Baba Yaga and shivered, though she did not feel so bad when she remembered the mouseykin out there in the shed in the yard.

The very next morning it happened. The old man went off to pay a visit to some friends of his in the next village. And as soon as the old man was out of sight the wicked stepmother called the little girl.

"You are to go to-day to your dear little aunt in the forest," says she, "and ask her for a needle and thread to mend a shirt."

"But here is a needle and thread," says the little girl.

"Hold your tongue," says the stepmother, and she gnashes her teeth, and they make a noise like clattering tongs. "Hold your tongue," she says. "Didn't I tell you you are to go to-day to your dear little aunt to ask for a needle and thread to mend a shirt?"

"How shall I find her?" says the little girl, nearly ready to cry, for she knew that her aunt was Baba Yaga, the bony-legged, the witch.

The stepmother took hold of the little girl's nose and pinched it.

"That is your nose," she says. "Can you feel it?"

"Yes," says the poor little girl.

"You must go along the road into the forest till you

come to a fallen tree; then you must turn to your left, and then follow your nose and you will find her," says the stepmother. "Now, be off with you, lazy one. Here is some food for you to eat by the way." She gave the little girl a bundle wrapped up in a towel.

The little girl wanted to go into the shed to tell the mouseykin she was going to Baba Yaga, and to ask what she should do. But she looked back, and there was the stepmother at the door watching her. So she had to go straight on.

She walked along the road through the forest till she came to the fallen tree. Then she turned to the left. Her nose was still hurting where the stepmother had pinched it, so she knew she had to go straight ahead. She was just setting out when she heard a little noise under the fallen tree.

"Scratch—scratch."

And out jumped the little mouse, and sat up in the road in front of her.

"O mouseykin, mouseykin," says the little girl, "my stepmother has sent me to her sister. And that is Baba Yaga, the bony-legged, the witch, and I do not know what to do."

"It will not be difficult," says the little mouse, "because of your kind heart. Take all the things you find in the road, and do with them what you like. Then you will escape from Baba Yaga, and everything will be well."

"Are you hungry, mouseykin?" said the little girl.

"I could nibble, I think," says the little mouse.

The little girl unfastened the towel, and there was nothing in it but stones. That was what the stepmother had given the little girl to eat by the way.

"Oh, I'm so sorry," says the little girl. "There's nothing for you to eat."

"Isn't there?" said mouseykin, and as she looked at them the little girl saw the stones turn to bread and jam. The little girl sat down on the fallen tree, and the little mouse sat beside her, and they ate bread and jam until they were not hungry any more.

"Keep the towel," says the little mouse; "I think it will be useful. And remember what I said about the things you find on the way. And now good-bye," says he.

"Good-bye," says the little girl, and runs along.

As she was running along she found a nice new handkerchief lying in the road. She picked it up and took it with her. Then she found a little bottle of oil. She picked it up and took it with her. Then she found some scraps of meat.

"Perhaps I'd better take them too," she said; and she took them.

Then she found a gay blue ribbon, and she took that. Then she found a little loaf of good bread, and she took that too.

"I daresay somebody will like it," she said.

And then she came to the hut of Baba Yaga, the bony-legged, the witch. There was a high fence round it with big gates. When she pushed them open they squeaked miserably, as if it hurt them to move. The little girl was sorry for them.

"How lucky," she says, "that I picked up the bottle of oil!" and she poured the oil into the hinges of the gates.

Inside the railing was Baba Yaga's hut, and it stood on hen's legs and walked about the yard. And in the yard there was standing Baba Yaga's servant, and she

Baba Yaga's hut stood on hen's legs and walked about the yard.

was crying bitterly because of the tasks Baba Yaga set her to do. She was crying bitterly and wiping her eyes on her petticoat.

"How lucky," says the little girl, "that I picked up a handkerchief!" And she gave the handkerchief to Baba Yaga's servant, who wiped her eyes on it and smiled through her tears.

Close by the hut was a huge dog, very thin, gnawing a dry crust.

"How lucky," says the little girl, "that I picked up a loaf!" And she gave the loaf to the dog, and he gobbled it up and licked his lips.

The little girl went bravely up to the hut and knocked on the door.

"Come in," says Baba Yaga.

The little girl went in, and there was Baba Yaga, the bony-legged, the witch, sitting weaving at a loom. In a corner of the hut was a thin black cat watching a mouse-hole.

"Good-day to you, auntie," says the little girl, trying not to tremble.

"Good-day to you, niece," says Baba Yaga.

"My stepmother has sent me to you to ask for a needle and thread to mend a shirt."

"Very well," says Baba Yaga, smiling, and showing her iron teeth. "You sit down here at the loom, and go on with my weaving, while I go and get you the needle and thread."

The little girl sat down at the loom and began to weave.

Baba Yaga went out and called to her servant, "Go,

make the bath hot and scrub my niece. Scrub her clean. I'll make a dainty meal of her."

The servant came in for the jug. The little girl begged her, "Be not too quick in making the fire, and carry the water in a sieve." The servant smiled, but said nothing, because she was afraid of Baba Yaga. But she took a very long time about getting the bath ready.

Baba Yaga came to the window and asked,—

"Are you weaving, little niece? Are you weaving, my pretty?"

"I am weaving, auntie," says the little girl.

When Baba Yaga went away from the window, the little girl spoke to the thin black cat who was watching the mouse-hole.

"What are you doing, thin black cat?"

"Watching for a mouse," says the thin black cat. "I haven't had any dinner for three days."

"How lucky," says the little girl, "that I picked up the scraps of meat!" And she gave them to the thin black cat. The thin black cat gobbled them up, and said to the little girl,—

"Little girl, do you want to get out of this?"

"Catkin dear," says the little girl, "I do want to get out of this, for Baba Yaga is going to eat me with her iron teeth."

"Well," says the cat, "I will help you."

Just then Baba Yaga came to the window.

"Are you weaving, little niece?" she asked. "Are you weaving, my pretty?"

"I am weaving, auntie," says the little girl, working away, while the loom went clickety clack, clickety clack.

Baba Yaga went away.

Says the thin black cat to the little girl: "You have a comb in your hair, and you have a towel. Take them and run for it while Baba Yaga is in the bath-house. When Baba Yaga chases after you, you must listen; and when she is close to you, throw away the towel, and it will turn into a big, wide river. It will take her a little time to get over that. But when she does, you must listen; and as soon as she is close to you throw away the comb, and it will sprout up into such a forest that she will never get through it at all."

"But she'll hear the loom stop," says the little girl.

"I'll see to that," says the thin black cat.

The cat took the little girl's place at the loom.

Clickety clack, clickety clack; the loom never stopped for a moment.

The little girl looked to see that Baba Yaga was in the bath-house, and then she jumped down from the little hut on hen's legs, and ran to the gates as fast as her legs could flicker.

The big dog leapt up to tear her to pieces. Just as he was going to spring on her he saw who she was.

"Why, this is the little girl who gave me the loaf," says he. "A good journey to you, little girl;" and he lay down again with his head between his paws.

When she came to the gates they opened quietly, quietly, without making any noise at all, because of the oil she had poured into their hinges.

Outside the gates there was a little birch tree that beat her in the eyes so that she could not go by.

"How lucky," says the little girl, "that I picked up the ribbon!" And she tied up the birch tree with the pretty blue ribbon. And the birch tree was so pleased with the ribbon that it stood still, admiring itself, and let the little girl go by.

How she did run!

Meanwhile the thin black cat sat at the loom. Clickety clack, clickety clack, sang the loom: but you never saw such a tangle as the tangle made by the thin black cat.

And presently Baba Yaga came to the window.

"Are you weaving, little niece?" she asked. "Are you weaving, my pretty?"

"I am weaving, auntie," says the thin black cat, tangling and tangling, while the loom went clickety clack, clickety clack.

"That's not the voice of my little dinner," says Baba Yaga, and she jumped into the hut, gnashing her iron teeth; and there was no little girl, but only the thin black cat, sitting at the loom, tangling and tangling the threads.

"Grr," says Baba Yaga, and jumps for the cat, and begins banging it about. "Why didn't you tear the little girl's eyes out?"

"In all the years I have served you," says the cat, "you have only given me one little bone; but the kind little girl gave me scraps of meat."

Baba Yaga threw the cat into a corner, and went out into the yard.

"Why didn't you squeak when she opened you?" she asked the gates.

"Why didn't you tear her to pieces?" she asked the dog.

"Why didn't you beat her in the face, and not let her go by?" she asked the birch tree.

"Why were you so long in getting the bath ready? If you had been quicker, she never would have got away," said Baba Yaga to the servant.

And she rushed about the yard, beating them all, and scolding at the top of her voice.

"Ah!" said the gates, "in all the years we have served you, you never even eased us with water; but the kind little girl poured good oil into our hinges."

"Ah!" said the dog, "in all the years I've served you, you never threw me anything but burnt crusts; but the kind little girl gave me a good loaf."

"Ah!" said the little birch tree, "in all the years I've served you, you never tied me up, even with thread; but the kind little girl tied me up with a gay blue ribbon."

"Ah!" said the servant, "in all the years I've served you, you have never given me even a rag; but the kind little girl gave me a pretty handkerchief."

Baba Yaga gnashed at them with her iron teeth. Then she jumped into the mortar and sat down. She drove it along with the pestle, and swept up her tracks with a besom, and flew off in pursuit of the little girl.

The little girl ran and ran. She put her ear to the ground and listened. Bang, bang, bangety bang! she could hear Baba Yaga beating the mortar with the pestle. Baba Yaga was quite close. There she was, beating with the pestle and sweeping with the besom, coming along the road.

As quickly as she could, the little girl took out the towel and threw it on the ground. And the towel grew bigger and bigger, and wetter and wetter, and there was a deep, broad river between Baba Yaga and the little girl.

The little girl turned and ran on. How she ran!

Baba Yaga came flying up in the mortar. But the mortar could not float in the river with Baba Yaga inside. She drove it in, but only got wet for her trouble. Tongs and pokers tumbling down a chimney are nothing to the noise she made as she gnashed her iron teeth. She turned home, and went flying back to the little hut on hen's legs. Then she got together all her cattle and drove them to the river.

"Drink, drink!" she screamed at them; and the cattle drank up all the river to the last drop. And Baba Yaga, sitting in the mortar, drove it with the pestle, and swept up her tracks with the besom, and flew over the dry bed of the river and on in pursuit of the little girl.

The little girl put her ear to the ground and listened. Bang, bang, bangety bang! She could hear Baba Yaga beating the mortar with the pestle. Nearer and nearer came the noise, and there was Baba Yaga, beating with the pestle and sweeping with the besom, coming along the road close behind.

The little girl threw down the comb, and it grew bigger and bigger, and its teeth sprouted up into a thick forest—so thick that not even Baba Yaga could force her way through. And Baba Yaga, gnashing her teeth and screaming with rage and disappointment, turned round and drove away home to her little hut on hen's legs.

The little girl ran on home. She was afraid to go in and see her stepmother, so she ran into the shed.

Scratch, scratch! Out came the little mouse.

"So you got away all right, my dear," says the little

mouse. "Now run in. Don't be afraid. Your father is back, and you must tell him all about it."

The little girl went into the house.

"Where have you been?" says her father; "and why are you so out of breath?"

The stepmother turned yellow when she saw her, and her eyes glowed, and her teeth ground together until they broke.

But the little girl was not afraid, and she went to her father and climbed on his knee, and told him everything just as it had happened. And when the old man knew that the stepmother had sent his little daughter to be eaten by Baba Yaga, he was so angry that he drove her out of the hut, and ever afterwards lived alone with the little girl. Much better it was for both of them.

The little mouse came and lived in the hut, and every day it used to sit up on the table and eat crumbs, and warm its paws on the little girl's glass of tea.

The Little Daughter of the Snow

THERE WERE once an old man and an old woman, his wife, and they lived together in a hut, in a village on the edge of the forest. There were many people in the village; quite a town it was—eight huts at least, thirty or forty souls, good company to be had for crossing the road. But the old man and the old woman were unhappy, in spite of living like that in the very middle of the world.

All the other huts had babies in them—yes, and little ones playing about in the road outside, and having to be shouted at when any one came driving by. But there were no babies in their hut, and the old woman never had to go to the door to see where her little one had strayed to, because she had no little one.

And these two, the old man and the old woman, used to stand whole hours, just peeping through their window to watch the children playing outside. They had dogs and a cat, and cocks and hens, but none of these made up for having no children. These two would just stand and watch the children of the other huts. The dogs would bark, but they took no notice; and the cat would curl up against them, but they never felt her; and as for the cocks and hens, well, they were fed, but that was all. The old people did not care for them, and spent all their time in watching the children who belonged to the other huts.

In the winter the children in their little sheepskin coats played in the crisp snow. They pelted each other with snowballs, and shouted and laughed, and then they rolled the snow together and made a snow woman—a regular snow Baba Yaga, a snow witch; such an old fright!

And the old man, watching from the window, saw this, and he says to the old woman,—

"Wife, let us go into the yard behind and make a little snow girl; and perhaps she will come alive, and be a little daughter to us."

"Husband," says the old woman, "there's no knowing what may be. Let us go into the yard and make a little snow girl."

So the two old people put on their big coats and their fur hats, and went out into the yard, where nobody could see them.

And they rolled up the snow, and began to make a little snow girl. Very, very tenderly they rolled up the snow to make her little arms and legs. The good God helped the old people, and their little snow girl was more beautiful than ever you could imagine. She was lovelier than a birch tree in spring.

Well, towards evening she was finished—a little girl, all snow, with blind white eyes, and a little mouth, with snow lips tightly closed.

"Oh, speak to us," says the old man.

"Won't you run about like the others, little white pigeon?" says the old woman.

And she did, you know, she really did.

Suddenly, in the twilight, they saw her eyes shining blue like the sky on a clear day. And her lips flushed and opened, and she smiled. And there were her little white teeth. And look, she had black hair, and it stirred in the wind.

She began dancing in the snow, like a little white spirit, tossing her long hair, and laughing softly to herself.

Wildly she danced, like snowflakes whirled in the wind. Her eyes shone, and her hair flew round her, and she sang, while the old people watched and wondered, and thanked God.

This is what she sang:—

> "No warm blood in me doth glow,
> Water in my veins doth flow;
> Yet I'll laugh and sing and play
> By frosty night and frosty day—
> Little daughter of the Snow.
>
> "But whenever I do know
> That you love me little, then
> I shall melt away again.
> Back into the sky I'll go—
> Little daughter of the Snow."

"God of mine, isn't she beautiful!" said the old man. "Run, wife, and fetch a blanket to wrap her in while you make clothes for her."

The old woman fetched a blanket, and put it round the shoulders of the little snow girl. And the old man picked her up, and she put her little cold arms round his neck.

"You must not keep me too warm," she said.

Well, they took her into the hut, and she lay on a bench in the corner farthest from the stove, while the old woman made her a little coat.

She began dancing in the snow, like a little white spirit.

The old man went out to buy a fur hat and boots from a neighbour for the little girl. The neighbour laughed at the old man; but a rouble is a rouble everywhere, and no one turns it from the door, and so he sold the old man a little fur hat, and a pair of little red boots with fur round the tops.

Then they dressed the little snow girl.

"Too hot, too hot," said the little snow girl. "I must go out into the cool night."

"But you must go to sleep now," said the old woman.

"By frosty night and frosty day," sang the little girl. "No; I will play by myself in the yard all night, and in the morning I'll play in the road with the children."

Nothing the old people said could change her mind.

"I am the little daughter of the Snow," she replied to everything, and she ran out into the yard into the snow.

How she danced and ran about in the moonlight on the white frozen snow!

The old people watched her and watched her. At last they went to bed; but more than once the old man got up in the night to make sure she was still there. And there she was, running about in the yard, chasing her shadow in the moonlight and throwing snowballs at the stars.

In the morning she came in, laughing, to have break-fast with the old people. She showed them how to make porridge for her, and that was very simple. They had only to take a piece of ice and crush it up in a little wooden bowl.

Then after breakfast she ran out in the road, to join the other children. And the old people watched her. Oh, proud they were, I can tell you, to see a little girl of

their own out there playing in the road! They fairly
longed for a sledge to come driving by, so that they
could run out into the road and call to the little snow
girl to be careful.

And the little snow girl played in the snow with the
other children. How she played! She could run faster
than any of them. Her little red boots flashed as she
ran about. Not one of the other children was a match
for her at snowballing. And when the children began
making a snow woman, a Baba Yaga, you would have
thought the little daughter of the Snow would have
died of laughing. She laughed and laughed, like ringing peals on little glass bells. But she helped in the
making of the snow woman, only laughing all the
time.

When it was done, all the children threw snowballs at
it, till it fell to pieces. And the little snow girl laughed
and laughed, and was so quick she threw more snowballs than any of them.

The old man and the old woman watched her, and
were very proud.

"She is all our own," said the old woman.

"Our little white pigeon," said the old man.

In the evening she had another bowl of ice-porridge,
and then she went off again to play by herself in the
yard.

"You'll be tired, my dear," says the old man.

"You'll sleep in the hut to-night, won't you, my love,"
says the old woman, "after running about all day long?"

But the little daughter of the Snow only laughed. "By
frosty night and frosty day," she sang, and ran out of
the door, laughing back at them with shining eyes.

And so it went on all through the winter. The little daughter of the Snow was singing and laughing and dancing all the time. She always ran out into the night and played by herself till dawn. Then she'd come in and have her ice-porridge. Then she'd play with the children. Then she'd have ice-porridge again, and off she would go, out into the night.

She was very good. She did everything the old woman told her. Only she would never sleep indoors. All the children of the village loved her. They did not know how they had ever played without her.

It went on so till just about this time of year. Perhaps it was a little earlier. Anyhow the snow was melting, and you could get about the paths. Often the children went together a little way into the forest in the sunny part of the day. The little snow girl went with them. It would have been no fun without her.

And then one day they went too far into the wood, and when they said they were going to turn back, little snow girl tossed her head under her little fur hat, and ran on laughing among the trees. The other children were afraid to follow her. It was getting dark. They waited as long as they dared, and then they ran home, holding each other's hands.

And there was the little daughter of the Snow out in the forest alone.

She looked back for the others, and could not see them. She climbed up into a tree; but the other trees were thick round her, and she could not see farther than when she was on the ground.

She called out from the tree,—

"Ai, ai, little friends, have pity on the little snow girl."

An old brown bear heard her, and came shambling up on his heavy paws.

"What are you crying about, little daughter of the Snow?"

"O big bear," says the little snow girl, "how can I help crying? I have lost my way, and dusk is falling, and all my little friends are gone."

"I will take you home," says the old brown bear.

"O big bear," says the little snow girl, "I am afraid of you. I think you would eat me. I would rather go home with some one else."

So the bear shambled away and left her.

An old gray wolf heard her, and came galloping up on his swift feet. He stood under the tree and asked,—

"What are you crying about, little daughter of the Snow?"

"O gray wolf," says the little snow girl, "how can I help crying? I have lost my way, and it is getting dark, and all my little friends are gone."

"I will take you home," says the old gray wolf.

"O gray wolf," says the little snow girl, "I am afraid of you. I think you would eat me. I would rather go home with some one else."

So the wolf galloped away and left her.

An old red fox heard her, and came running up to the tree on his little pads. He called out cheerfully,—

"What are you crying about, little daughter of the Snow?"

"O red fox," says the little snow girl, "how can I help crying? I have lost my way, and it is quite dark, and all my little friends are gone."

"I will take you home," says the old red fox.

"O red fox," says the little snow girl, "I am not afraid of you. I do not think you will eat me. I will go home with you, if you will take me."

So she scrambled down from the tree, and she held the fox by the hair of his back, and they ran together through the dark forest. Presently they saw the lights in the windows of the huts, and in a few minutes they were at the door of the hut that belonged to the old man and the old woman.

And there were the old man and the old woman, crying and lamenting.

"Oh, what has become of our little snow girl?"

"Oh, where is our little white pigeon?"

"Here I am," says the little snow girl. "The kind red fox has brought me home. You must shut up the dogs."

The old man shut up the dogs.

"We are very grateful to you," says he to the fox.

"Are you really?" says the old red fox; "for I am very hungry."

"Here is a nice crust for you," says the old woman.

"Oh," says the fox, "but what I would like would be a nice plump hen. After all, your little snow girl is worth a nice plump hen."

"Very well," says the old woman, but she grumbles to her husband.

"Husband," says she, "we have our little girl again."

"We have," says he; "thanks be for that."

"It seems a waste to give away a good plump hen."

"It does," says he.

"Well, I was thinking," says the old woman, and then she tells him what she meant to do. And he went off and got two sacks.

In one sack they put a fine plump hen, and in the other they put the fiercest of the dogs. They took the bags outside and called to the fox. The old red fox came up to them, licking his lips, because he was so hungry.

They opened one sack, and out the hen fluttered. The old red fox was just going to seize her, when they opened the other sack, and out jumped the fierce dog. The poor fox saw his eyes flashing in the dark, and was so frightened that he ran all the way back into the deep forest, and never had the hen at all.

"That was well done," said the old man and the old woman. "We have got our little snow girl, and not had to give away our plump hen."

Then they heard the little snow girl singing in the hut. This is what she sang:—

> "Old ones, old ones, now I know
> Less you love me than a hen,
> I shall go away again.
> Good-bye, ancient ones, good-bye,
> Back I go across the sky;
> To my motherkin I go—
> Little daughter of the Snow."

They ran into the house. There were a little pool of water in front of the stove, and a fur hat, and a little coat, and little red boots were lying in it. And yet it seemed to the old man and the old woman that they saw the little snow girl, with her bright eyes and her long hair, dancing in the room.

"Do not go! do not go!" they begged, and already they could hardly see the little dancing girl.

But they heard her laughing, and they heard her song:—

> "Old ones, old ones, now I know
> Less you love me than a hen,
> I shall melt away again.
> To my motherkin I go—
> Little daughter of the Snow."

And just then the door blew open from the yard, and a cold wind filled the room, and the little daughter of the Snow was gone.

The little snow girl leapt into the arms of Frost her father and Snow her mother, and they carried her away over the stars to the far north, and there she plays all through the summer on the frozen seas. In winter she comes back to Russia, and some day, you know, when you are making a snow woman, you may find the little daughter of the Snow standing there instead.

The Golden Fish

L ONG AGO, near the shore of the blue sea, an old
man lived with his old woman in a little old hut
made of earth and moss and logs. They never had a
rouble to spend. A rouble! they never had a kopeck.
They just lived there in the little hut, and the old man
caught fish out of the sea in his old net, and the old
woman cooked the fish; and so they lived, poorly
enough in summer and worse in winter. Sometimes
they had a few fish to sell, but not often. In the summer
evenings they sat outside their hut on a broken old
bench, and the old man mended the holes in his ragged
old net. There were holes in it a hare could jump
through with his ears standing, let alone one of those
little fishes that live in the sea. The old woman sat on
the bench beside him, and patched his trousers and
complained.

Well, one day the old man went fishing, as he always
did. All day long he fished, and caught nothing. And
then in the evening, when he was thinking he might as
well give up and go home, he threw his net for the last
time, and when he came to pull it in he began to think
he had caught an island instead of a haul of fish, and a
strong and lively island at that—the net was so heavy
and pulled so hard against his feeble old arms.

"This time," says he, "I have caught a hundred fish at
least."

Not a bit of it. The net came in as heavy as if it were full of fighting fish, but seemed to be empty.

But it was not quite empty, for when the last of the net came ashore there was something glittering in it— a golden fish, not very big and not very little, caught in the meshes. And it was this single golden fish which had made the net so heavy.

The old fisherman took the golden fish in his hands.

"At least it will be enough for supper," said he.

But the golden fish lay still in his hands, and looked at him with wise eyes, and spoke—yes, it spoke, just as if it were you or I.

"Old man," says the fish, "do not kill me. I beg you throw me back into the blue waters. Some day I may be able to be of use to you."

"What?" says the old fisherman; "and do you talk with a human voice?"

"I do," says the fish. "And my fish's heart feels pain like yours. It would be as bitter to me to die as it would be to yourself."

"And is that so?" says the old fisherman. "Well, you shall not die this time." And he threw the golden fish back into the sea.

You would have thought the golden fish would have splashed with his tail, and turned head downwards, and swum away into the blue depths of the sea. Not a bit of it. It stayed there with its tail slowly flapping in the water so as to keep its head up, and it looked at the fisherman with its wise eyes, and it spoke again.

"You have given me my life," says the golden fish. "Now ask anything you wish from me, and you shall have it."

The old fisherman stood there on the shore, combing his beard with his old fingers, and thinking. Think as he would, he could not call to mind a single thing he wanted.

"No, fish," he said at last; "I think I have everything I need."

"Well, if ever you do want anything, come and ask for it," says the fish, and turns over, flashing gold, and goes down into the blue sea.

The old fisherman went back to his hut, where his wife was waiting for him.

"What!" she screamed out; "you haven't caught so much as one little fish for our supper?"

"I caught one fish, mother," says the old man: "a golden fish it was, and it spoke to me; and I let it go, and it told me to ask for anything I wanted."

"And what did you ask for? Show me."

"I couldn't think of anything to ask for; so I did not ask for anything at all."

"Fool," says his wife, "and dolt, and us with no food to put in our mouths. Go back at once, and ask for some bread."

Well, the poor old fisherman got down his net, and tramped back to the seashore. And he stood on the shore of the wide blue sea, and he called out,—

> "Head in air and tail in sea,
> Fish, fish, listen to me."

And in a moment there was the golden fish with his head out of the water, flapping his tail below him in the water, and looking at the fisherman with his wise eyes.

"What is it?" said the fish.

"Be so kind," says the fisherman; "be so kind. We have no bread in the house."

"Go home," says the fish, and turned over and went down into the sea.

"God be good to me," says the old fisherman; "but what shall I say to my wife, going home like this without the bread?" And he went home very wretchedly, and slower than he came.

As soon as he came within sight of his hut he saw his wife, and she was waving her arms and shouting.

"Stir your old bones," she screamed out. "It's as fine a loaf as ever I've seen."

And he hurried along, and found his old wife cutting up a huge loaf of white bread, mind you, not black—a huge loaf of white bread, nearly as big as a child.

"You did not do so badly after all," said his old wife as they sat there with the samovar on the table between them, dipping their bread in the hot tea.

But that night, as they lay sleeping on the stove, the old woman poked the old man in the ribs with her bony elbow. He groaned and woke up.

"I've been thinking," says his wife, "your fish might have given us a trough to keep the bread in while he was about it. There is a lot left over, and without a trough it will go bad, and not be fit for anything. And our old trough is broken; besides, it's too small. First thing in the morning off you go, and ask your fish to give us a new trough to put the bread in."

Early in the morning she woke the old man again, and he had to get up and go down to the seashore. He was very much afraid, because he thought the fish would not take it kindly. But at dawn, just as the red sun was rising out of the sea, he stood on the shore, and called out in his windy old voice,—

> "Head in air and tail in sea,
> Fish, fish, listen to me."

And there in the morning sunlight was the golden fish, looking at him with its wise eyes.

"I beg your pardon," says the old man, "but could you, just to oblige my wife, give us some sort of trough to put the bread in?"

"Go home," says the fish; and down it goes into the blue sea.

The old man went home, and there, outside the hut, was the old woman, looking at the handsomest bread trough that ever was seen on earth. Painted it was, with little flowers, in three colours, and there were strips of gilding about its handles.

"Look at this," grumbled the old woman. "This is far too fine a trough for a tumble-down hut like ours. Why, there is scarcely a place in the roof where the rain does not come through. If we were to keep this trough in such a hut, it would be spoiled in a month. You must go back to your fish and ask it for a new hut."

"I hardly like to do that," says the old man.

"Get along with you," says his wife. "If the fish can make a trough like this, a hut will be no trouble to him. And, after all, you must not forget he owes his life to you."

"I suppose that is true," says the old man; but he went back to the shore with a heavy heart. He stood on the edge of the sea and called out, doubtfully,—

"Head in air and tail in sea,
Fish, fish, listen to me."

Instantly there was a ripple in the water, and the golden fish was looking at him with its wise eyes.

"Well?" says the fish.

"My old woman is so pleased with the trough that she wants a new hut to keep it in, because ours, if you could only see it, is really falling to pieces, and the rain comes in and——"

"Go home," says the fish.

The old fisherman went home, but he could not find his old hut at all. At first he thought he had lost his way. But then he saw his wife. And she was walking about, first one way and then the other, looking at the finest hut that God ever gave a poor moujik to keep him from the rain and the cold, and the too great heat of the sun. It was built of sound logs, neatly finished at the ends and carved. And the overhanging of the roof was cut in patterns, so neat, so pretty, you could never think how they had been done. The old woman looked at it from all sides. And the old man stood, wondering. Then they went in together. And everything within the hut was new and clean. There were a fine big stove, and strong wooden benches, and a good table, and a fire lit in the stove, and logs ready to put in, and a samovar already on the boil—a fine new samovar of glittering brass.

You would have thought the old woman would have been satisfied with that. Not a bit of it.

"You don't know how to lift your eyes from the ground," says she. "You don't know what to ask. I am tired of being a peasant woman and a moujik's wife. I was made for something better. I want to be a lady, and have good people to do the work, and see folk bow and curtsy to me when I meet them walking abroad. Go back at once to the fish, you old fool, and ask him for that, instead of bothering him for little trifles like bread troughs and moujiks' huts. Off with you."

The old fisherman went back to the shore with a sad heart; but he was afraid of his wife, and he dared not disobey her. He stood on the shore, and called out in his windy old voice,—

"Head in air and tail in sea,
Fish, fish, listen to me."

Instantly there was the golden fish looking at him with its wise eyes.

"Well?" says the fish.

"My old woman won't give me a moment's peace," says the old man; "and since she has the new hut— which is a fine one, I must say; as good a hut as ever I saw—she won't be content at all. She is tired of being a peasant's wife, and wants to be a lady with a house and servants, and to see the good folk curtsy to her when she meets them walking abroad."

"Go home," says the fish.

The old man went home, thinking about the hut, and how pleasant it would be to live in it, even if his wife were a lady.

But when he got home the hut had gone, and in its place there was a fine brick house, three stories high. There were servants running this way and that in the courtyard. There was a cook in the kitchen, and there was his old woman, in a dress of rich brocade, sitting idle in a tall carved chair, and giving orders right and left.

"Good health to you, wife," says the old man.

"Ah, you, clown that you are, how dare you call me your wife! Can't you see that I'm a lady? Here! Off with this fellow to the stables, and see that he gets a beating he won't forget in a hurry."

Instantly the servants seized the old man by the collar and lugged him along to the stables. There the grooms treated him to such a whipping that he could hardly stand on his feet. After that the old woman made him doorkeeper. She ordered that a besom should be given him to clean up the court-yard, and said that he was to have his meals in the kitchen. A wretched life the old man lived. All day long he was sweeping up the courtyard, and if there was a speck of dirt to be seen in it anywhere, he paid for it at once in the stable under the whips of the grooms.

Time went on, and the old woman grew tired of being only a lady. And at last there came a day when she sent into the yard to tell the old man to come before her. The poor old man combed his hair and cleaned his boots, and came into the house, and bowed low before the old woman.

"Be off with you, you old good-for-nothing!" says she. "Go and find your golden fish, and tell him from me that I am tired of being a lady. I want to be Tzaritza, with generals and courtiers and men of state to do whatever I tell them."

The old man went along to the seashore, glad enough to be out of the courtyard and out of reach of the stablemen with their whips. He came to the shore, and cried out in his windy old voice,—

"Head in air and tail in sea,
Fish, fish, listen to me."

And there was the golden fish looking at him with its wise eyes.

"What's the matter now, old man?" says the fish.

"My old woman is going on worse than ever," says the old fisherman. "My back is sore with the whips of her grooms. And now she says it isn't enough for her to be a lady; she wants to be a Tzaritza."

"Never you worry about it," says the fish. "Go home and praise God;" and with that the fish turned over and went down into the sea.

The old man went home slowly, for he did not know what his wife would do to him if the golden fish did not make her into a Tzaritza.

But as soon as he came near he heard the noise of trumpets and the beating of drums, and there where the fine stone house had been was now a great palace with a golden roof. Behind it was a big garden of flowers, that are fair to look at but have no fruit, and before it was a meadow of fine green grass. And on the meadow was an army of soldiers drawn up in squares and all dressed alike. And suddenly the fisherman saw his old woman in the gold and silver dress of a Tzaritza come stalking out on the balcony with her generals and boyars to hold a review of her troops. And the drums beat and the trumpets sounded, and the soldiers cried "Hurrah!" And the poor old fisherman found a dark corner in one of the barns, and lay down in the straw.

Time went on, and at last the old woman was tired of being Tzaritza. She thought she was made for something better. And one day she said to her chamberlain,—

"Find me that ragged old beggar who is always hanging about in the courtyard. Find him, and bring him here."

The chamberlain told his officers, and the officers told the servants, and the servants looked for the old man, and found him at last asleep on the straw in the corner of one of the barns. They took some of the dirt off him, and brought him before the Tzaritza, sitting proudly on her golden throne.

"Listen, old fool!" says she. "Be off to your golden fish, and tell it I am tired of being Tzaritza. Anybody can be Tzaritza. I want to be the ruler of the seas, so that all the waters shall obey me, and all the fishes shall be my servants."

"I don't like to ask that," said the old man, trembling.

"What's that?" she screamed at him. "Do you dare to answer the Tzaritza? If you do not set off this minute, I'll have your head cut off and your body thrown to the dogs."

Unwillingly the old man hobbled off. He came to the shore, and cried out with a windy, quavering old voice,—

> "Head in air and tail in sea,
> Fish, fish, listen to me."

Nothing happened.

The old man thought of his wife, and what would

happen to him if she were still Tzaritza when he came home. Again he called out,—

"Head in air and tail in sea,
Fish, fish, listen to me."

Nothing happened, nothing at all.

A third time, with the tears running down his face, he called out in his windy, creaky, quavering old voice,—

"Head in air and tail in sea,
Fish, fish, listen to me."

Suddenly there was a loud noise, louder and louder over the sea. The sun hid itself. The sea broke into waves, and the waves piled themselves one upon another. The sky and the sea turned black, and there was a great roaring wind that lifted the white crests of the waves and tossed them abroad over the waters. The golden fish came up out of the storm and spoke out of the sea.

"What is it now?" says he, in a voice more terrible than the voice of the storm itself.

"O fish," says the old man, trembling like a reed shaken by the storm, "my old woman is worse than before. She is tired of being Tzaritza. She wants to be the ruler of the seas, so that all the waters shall obey her and all the fishes be her servants."

The golden fish said nothing, nothing at all. He turned over and went down into the deep seas. And the wind from the sea was so strong that the old man could hardly stand against it. For a long time he waited, afraid to go home; but at last the storm calmed, and it grew towards evening, and he hobbled back, thinking to creep in and hide amongst the straw.

As he came near, he listened for the trumpets and the drums. He heard nothing except the wind from the sea rustling the little leaves of birch trees. He looked for the palace. It was gone, and where it had been was a little tumbledown hut of earth and logs. It seemed to the old fisherman that he knew that little hut, and he looked at it with joy. And he went to the door of the hut, and there was sitting his old woman in a ragged dress, cleaning out a saucepan, and singing in a creaky old voice. And this time she was glad to see him, and they sat down together on the bench and drank tea without sugar, because they had not any money.

They began to live again as they used to live, and the old man grew happier every day. He fished and fished, and many were the fish that he caught, and of many kinds; but never again did he catch another golden fish that could talk like a human being. I doubt whether he would have said anything to his wife about it, even if he had caught one every day.

Alenoushka and Her Brother

ONCE UPON a time there were two orphan children, a little boy and a little girl. Their father and mother were dead, and they were alone. The little boy was called Vanoushka,* and the little girl's name was Alenoushka.*

They set out together to walk through the whole of the great wide world. It was a long journey they set out on, and they did not think of any end to it, but only of moving on and on, and never stopping long enough in one place to be unhappy there.

They were travelling one day over a broad plain, padding along on their little bare feet. There were no trees on the plain, no bushes; open flat country as far as you could see, and the great sun up in the sky burning the grass and making their throats dry, and the sandy ground so hot that they could scarcely bear to set their feet on it. All day from early morning they had been walking, and the heat grew greater and greater towards noon.

"Oh," said little Vanoushka, "my throat is so dry. I want a drink. I must have a drink—just a little drink of cool water."

*Vanoushka and Alenoushka are affectionate forms of Ivan and Elena.

"We must go on," said Alenoushka, "till we come to a well. Then we will drink."

They went on along the track, with their eyes burning and their throats as dry as sand on a stove.

But presently Vanoushka cried out joyfully. He saw a horse's hoofmark in the ground. And it was full of water, like a little well.

"Sister, sister," says he, "the horse has made a little well for me with his great hoof, and now we can have a drink; and oh, but I am thirsty!"

"Not yet, brother," says Alenoushka. "If you drink from the hoofmark of a horse, you will turn into a little foal, and that would never do."

"I am so very thirsty," says Vanoushka; but he did as his sister told him, and they walked on together under the burning sun.

A little farther on Vanoushka saw the hoofmark of a cow, and there was water in it glittering in the sun.

"Sister, sister," says Vanoushka, "the cow has made a little well for me, and now I can have a drink."

"Not yet, brother," says Alenoushka. "If you drink from the hoofmark of a cow, you will turn into a little calf, and that would never do. We must go on till we come to a well. There we will drink and rest ourselves. There will be trees by the well, and shadows, and we will lie down there by the quiet water and cool our hands and feet, and perhaps our eyes will stop burning."

So they went on farther along the track that scorched the bare soles of their feet, and under the sun that burned their heads and their little bare necks. The sun was high in the sky above them, and it seemed to Vanoushka that they would never come to the well.

But when they had walked on and on, and he was nearly crying with thirst, only that the sun had dried up all his tears and burnt them before they had time to come into his eyes, he saw another footprint. It was quite a tiny footprint, divided in the middle—the footprint of a sheep; and in it was a little drop of clear water, sparkling in the sun. He said nothing to his sister, nothing at all. But he went down on his hands and knees and drank that water, that little drop of clear water, to cool his burning throat. And he had no sooner drunk it than he had turned into a little lamb who ran round and round Alenoushka, frisking and leaping, with its little tail tossing in the air.

Alenoushka looked round for her brother, but could not see him. But there was the little lamb, leaping round her, trying to lick her face, and there in the ground was the print left by the sheep's foot.

She guessed at once what had happened, and burst into tears. There was a hayrick close by, and under the hayrick Alenoushka sat down and wept. The little lamb, seeing her so sad, stood gravely in front of her; but not for long, for he was a little lamb, and he could not help himself. However sad he felt, he had to leap and frisk in the sun, and toss his little white tail.

Presently a fine gentleman came riding by on his big black horse. He stopped when he came to the hayrick. He was very much surprised at seeing a beautiful little girl sitting there, crying her eyes out, while a white lamb frisked this way and that, and played before her, and now and then ran up to her and licked the tears from her face with its little pink tongue.

"What is your name," says the fine gentleman, "and

why are you in trouble? Perhaps I may be able to help you."

"My name is Alenoushka, and this is my little brother Vanoushka, whom I love." And she told him the whole story.

"Well, I can hardly believe all that," says the fine gentleman. "But come with me, and I will dress you in fine clothes, and set silver ornaments in your hair, and bracelets of gold on your little brown wrists. And as for the lamb, he shall come too, if you love him. Wherever you are there he shall be, and you shall never be parted from him."

And so Alenoushka took her little brother in her arms, and the fine gentleman lifted them up before him on the big black horse, and galloped home with them across the plain to his big house not far from the river. And when he got home he made a feast and married Alenoushka, and they lived together so happily that good people rejoiced to see them, and bad ones were jealous. And the little lamb lived in the house, and never grew any bigger, but always frisked and played, and followed Alenoushka wherever she went.

And then one day, when the fine gentleman had ridden far away to the town to buy a new bracelet for Alenoushka, there came an old witch. Ugly she was, with only one tooth in her head, and wicked as ever went about the world doing evil to decent folk. She begged from Alenoushka, and said she was hungry, and Alenoushka begged her to share her dinner. And she put a spell in the wine that Alenoushka drank, so that Alenoushka fell ill, and before evening, when the fine

Ugly she was, with only one tooth in her head.

gentleman came riding back, had become pale, pale as snow, and as thin as an old stick.

"My dear," says the fine gentleman, "what is the matter with you?"

"Perhaps I shall be better to-morrow," says Alenoushka.

Well, the next day the gentleman rode into the fields, and the old hag came again while he was out.

"Would you like me to cure you?" says she. "I know a way to make you as well as ever you were. Plump you will be, and pretty again, before your husband comes riding home."

"And what must I do?" says Alenoushka, crying to think herself so ugly.

"You must go to the river and bathe this afternoon," says the old witch. "I will be there and put a spell on the water. Secretly you must go, for if any one knows whither you have gone my spell will not work."

So Alenoushka wrapped a shawl about her head, and slipped out of the house and went to the river. Only the little lamb, Vanoushka, knew where she had gone. He followed her, leaping about, and tossing his little white tail. The old witch was waiting for her. She sprang out of the bushes by the riverside, and seized Alenoushka, and tore off her pretty white dress, and fastened a heavy stone about her neck, and threw her from the bank into a deep place, so that she sank to the bottom of the river. Then the old witch, the wicked hag, put on Alenoushka's pretty white dress, and cast a spell, and made herself so like Alenoushka to look at that nobody could tell the difference. Only the little lamb had seen everything that had happened.

The fine gentleman came riding home in the evening, and he rejoiced when he saw his dear Alenoushka well again, with plump pink cheeks, and a smile on her rosy lips.

But the little lamb knew everything. He was sad and melancholy, and would not eat, and went every morning and every evening to the river, and there wandered about the banks, and cried, "Baa, baa," and was answered by the sighing of the wind in the long reeds.

The witch saw that the lamb went off by himself every morning and every evening. She watched where he went, and when she knew she began to hate the lamb; and she gave orders for the sticks to be cut, and the iron cauldron to be heated, and the steel knives made sharp. She sent a servant to catch the lamb; and she said to the fine gentleman, who thought all the time that she was Alenoushka, "It is time for the lamb to be killed, and made into a tasty stew."

The fine gentleman was astonished.

"What," says he, "you want to have the lamb killed? Why, you called it your brother when first I found you by the hayrick in the plain. You were always giving it caresses and sweet words. You loved it so much that I was sick of the sight of it, and now you give orders for its throat to be cut. Truly," says he, "the mind of woman is like the wind in summer."

The lamb ran away when he saw that the servant had come to catch him. He heard the sharpening of the knives, and had seen the cutting of the wood, and the great cauldron taken from its place. He was frightened, and he ran away, and came to the river bank, where the wind was sighing through the tall reeds. And there he sang a farewell song to his sister, thinking he had not long to live. The servant followed the lamb cunningly, and crept near to catch him, and heard his little song. This is what he sang:—

"Alenoushka, little sister,
 They are going to slaughter me;
 They are cutting wooden fagots,
 They are heating iron cauldrons,
 They are sharpening knives of steel."

And Alenoushka, lamenting, answered the lamb from the bottom of the river:—

"O my brother Ivanoushka,
 A heavy stone is round my throat,
 Silken grass grows through my fingers,
 Yellow sand lies on my breast."

The servant listened, and marvelled at the miracle of the lamb singing, and the sweet voice answering him from the river. He crept away quietly, and came to the fine gentleman, and told him what he had heard; and they set out together to the river, to watch the lamb, and listen, and see what was happening.

The little white lamb stood on the bank of the river weeping, so that his tears fell into the water. And presently he sang again:—

"Alenoushka, little sister,
 They are going to slaughter me;
 They are cutting wooden fagots,
 They are heating iron cauldrons,
 They are sharpening knives of steel."

And Alenoushka answered him, lamenting, from the bottom of the river:—

"O my brother Ivanoushka,
A heavy stone is round my throat,
Silken grass grows through my fingers,
Yellow sand lies on my breast."

The fine gentleman heard, and he was sure that the voice was the voice of his own dear wife, and he remembered how she had loved the lamb. He sent his servant to fetch men, and fishing nets and nets of silk. The men came running, and they dragged the river with fishing nets, and brought their nets empty to land. Then they tried with nets of fine silk, and, as they drew them in, there was Alenoushka lying in the nets as if she were asleep.

They brought her to the bank and untied the stone from her white neck, and washed her in fresh water and clothed her in white clothes. But they had no sooner done all this than she woke up, more beautiful than ever she had been before, though then she was pretty enough, God knows. She woke, and sprang up, and threw her arms round the neck of the little white lamb, who suddenly became once more her little brother Vanoushka, who had been so thirsty as to drink water from the hoofmark of a sheep. And Vanoushka laughed and shouted in the sunshine, and the fine gentleman wept tears of joy. And they all praised God and kissed each other, and went home together, and began to live as happily as before, even more happily, because Vanoushka was no longer a lamb. But as soon as they got home the fine gentleman turned the old witch out of the house. And she became an ugly old hag, and went away to the deep woods, shrieking as she went.

Vanoushka grew up as handsome as Alenoushka was pretty. And he became a great hunter. And he married the sister of the fine gentleman. And they all lived happily together, and ate honey every day, with white bread and new milk.

Prince Ivan

ONCE UPON a time, very long ago, there was a little Prince Ivan who was dumb. Never a word had he spoken from the day that he was born—not so much as a "Yes" or a "No," or a "Please" or a "Thank you." A great sorrow he was to his father because he could not speak. Indeed, neither his father nor his mother could bear the sight of him, for they thought, "A poor sort of Tzar will a dumb boy make!" They even prayed, and said, "If only we could have another child, whatever it is like, it could be no worse than this tongue-tied brat who cannot say a word." And for that wish they were punished, as you shall hear. And they took no sort of care of the little Prince Ivan, and he spent all his time in the stables, listening to the tales of an old groom.

He was a wise man was the old groom, and he knew the past and the future, and what was happening under the earth. Maybe he had learnt his wisdom from the horses. Anyway, he knew more than other folk, and there came a day when he said to Prince Ivan,—

"Little Prince," says he, "to-day you have a sister, and a bad one at that. She has come because of your father's prayers and your mother's wishes. A witch she is, and she will grow like a seed of corn. In six weeks she'll be a grown witch, and with her iron teeth she will eat up your father, and eat up your mother, and eat up

91

you too, if she gets the chance. There's no saving the old people; but if you are quick, and do what I tell you, you may escape, and keep your soul in your body. And I love you, my little dumb Prince, and do not wish to think of your little body between her iron teeth. You must go to your father and ask him for the best horse he has, and then gallop like the wind, and away to the end of the world."

The little Prince ran off and found his father. There was his father, and there was his mother, and a little baby girl was in his mother's arms, screaming like a little fury.

"Well, she's not dumb," said his father, as if he were well pleased.

"Father," says the little Prince, "may I have the fastest horse in the stable?" And those were the first words that ever left his mouth.

"What!" says his father, "have you got a voice at last? Yes, take whatever horse you want. And see, you have a little sister; a fine little girl she is too. She has teeth already. It's a pity they are black, but time will put that right, and it's better to have black teeth than to be born dumb."

Little Prince Ivan shook in his shoes when he heard of the black teeth of his little sister, for he knew that they were iron. He thanked his father and ran off to the stable. The old groom saddled the finest horse there was. Such a horse you never saw. Black it was, and its saddle and bridle were trimmed with shining silver. And little Prince Ivan climbed up and sat on the great black horse, and waved his hand to the old groom, and galloped away, on and on over the wide world.

"It's a big place, this world," thought the little Prince. "I wonder when I shall come to the end of it." You see, he had never been outside the palace grounds. And he had only ridden a little Finnish pony. And now he sat high up, perched on the back of the great black horse, who galloped with hoofs that thundered beneath him, and leapt over rivers and streams and hillocks, and anything else that came in his way.

On and on galloped the little Prince on the great black horse. There were no houses anywhere to be seen. It was a long time since they had passed any people, and little Prince Ivan began to feel very lonely, and to wonder if indeed he had come to the end of the world, and could bring his journey to an end.

Suddenly, on a wide, sandy plain, he saw two old, old women sitting in the road.

They were bent double over their work, sewing and sewing, and now one and now the other broke a needle, and took a new one out of a box between them, and threaded the needle with thread from another box, and went on sewing and sewing. Their old noses nearly touched their knees as they bent over their work.

Little Prince Ivan pulled up the great black horse in a cloud of dust, and spoke to the old women.

"Grandmothers," said he, "is this the end of the world? Let me stay here and live with you, and be safe from my baby sister, who is a witch and has iron teeth. Please let me stay with you, and I'll be very little trouble, and thread your needles for you when you break them."

"Prince Ivan, my dear," said one of the old women, "this is not the end of the world, and little good would it be to you to stay with us. For as soon as we have broken all our needles and used up all our thread we shall die, and then where would you be? Your sister with the iron teeth would have you in a minute."

The little Prince cried bitterly, for he was very little and all alone. He rode on further over the wide world, the black horse galloping and galloping, and throwing the dust from his thundering hoofs.

He came into a forest of great oaks, the biggest oak trees in the whole world. And in that forest was a dreadful noise—the crashing of trees falling, the breaking of branches, and the whistling of things hurled through the air. The Prince rode on, and there before him was the huge giant, Tree-rooter, hauling the great oaks out of the ground and flinging them aside like weeds.

"I should be safe with him," thought little Prince Ivan, "and this, surely, must be the end of the world."

He rode close up under the giant, and stopped the black horse, and shouted up into the air.

"Please, great giant," says he, "is this the end of the world? And may I live with you and be safe from my sister, who is a witch, and grows like a seed of corn, and has iron teeth?"

"Prince Ivan, my dear," says Tree-rooter, "this is not the end of the world, and little good would it be to you to stay with me. For as soon as I have rooted up all these trees I shall die, and then where would you be? Your sister would have you in a minute. And already there are not many big trees left."

And the giant set to work again, pulling up the great trees and throwing them aside. The sky was full of flying trees.

Little Prince Ivan cried bitterly, for he was very little and was all alone. He rode on further over the wide world, the black horse galloping and galloping under the tall trees, and throwing clods of earth from his thundering hoofs.

He came among the mountains. And there was a roaring and a crashing in the mountains as if the earth was falling to pieces. One after another whole mountains were lifted up into the sky and flung down to earth, so that they broke and scattered into dust. And the big black horse galloped through the mountains, and little Prince Ivan sat bravely on his back. And there, close before him, was the huge giant Mountain-tosser, picking up the mountains like pebbles and hurling them to little pieces and dust upon the ground.

"This must be the end of the world," thought the little Prince; "and at any rate I should be safe with him."

"Please, great giant," says he, "is this the end of the world? And may I live with you and be safe from my sister, who is a witch, and has iron teeth, and grows like a seed of corn?"

"Prince Ivan, my dear," says Mountain-tosser, resting for a moment and dusting the rocks off his great hands, "this is not the end of the world, and little good would it be to you to stay with me. For as soon as I have picked up all these mountains and thrown them down again I shall die, and then where would you be? Your sister would have you in a minute. And there are not very many mountains left."

And the giant set to work again, lifting up the great mountains and hurling them away. The sky was full of flying mountains.

Little Prince Ivan wept bitterly, for he was very little and was all alone. He rode on further over the wide world, the black horse galloping and galloping along the mountain paths, and throwing the stones from his thundering hoofs.

At last he came to the end of the world, and there, hanging in the sky above him, was the castle of the little sister of the Sun. Beautiful it was, made of cloud, and hanging in the sky, as if it were built of red roses.

"I should be safe up there," thought little Prince Ivan, and just then the Sun's little sister opened the window and beckoned to him.

Prince Ivan patted the big black horse and whispered to it, and it leapt up high into the air and through the window, into the very courtyard of the castle.

"Stay here and play with me," said the little sister of the Sun; and Prince Ivan tumbled off the big black horse into her arms, and laughed because he was so happy.

Merry and pretty was the Sun's little sister, and she was very kind to little Prince Ivan. They played games together, and when she was tired she let him do whatever he liked and run about her castle. This way and that he ran about the battlements of rosy cloud, hanging in the sky over the end of the world.

But one day he climbed up and up to the topmost turret of the castle. From there he could see the whole world. And far, far away, beyond the mountains, beyond the forests, beyond the wide plains, he saw his father's palace where he had been born. The roof of the palace was gone, and the walls were broken and crumbling. And little Prince Ivan came slowly down from the turret, and his eyes were red with weeping.

"My dear," says the Sun's little sister, "why are your eyes so red?"

"It is the wind up there," says little Prince Ivan.

And the Sun's little sister put her head out of the window of the castle of cloud and whispered to the winds not to blow so hard.

But next day little Prince Ivan went up again to that topmost turret, and looked far away over the wide world to the ruined palace. "She has eaten them all with her iron teeth," he said to himself. And his eyes were red when he came down.

"My dear," says the Sun's little sister, "your eyes are red again."

"It is the wind," says little Prince Ivan.

And the Sun's little sister put her head out of the window and scolded the wind.

But the third day again little Prince Ivan climbed up the stairs of cloud to that topmost turret, and looked far away to the broken palace where his father and mother had lived. And he came down from the turret with the tears running down his face.

"Why, you are crying, my dear!" says the Sun's little sister. "Tell me what it is all about."

So little Prince Ivan told the little sister of the Sun how his sister was a witch, and how he wept to think of his father and mother, and how he had seen the ruins of his father's palace far away, and how he could not stay with her happily until he knew how it was with his parents.

"Perhaps it is not yet too late to save them from her

iron teeth, though the old groom said that she would certainly eat them, and that it was the will of God. But let me ride back on my big black horse."

"Do not leave me, my dear," says the Sun's little sister. "I am lonely here by myself."

"I will ride back on my big black horse, and then I will come to you again."

"What must be, must," says the Sun's little sister; "though she is more likely to eat you than you are to save them. You shall go. But you must take with you a magic comb, a magic brush, and two apples of youth. These apples would make young once more the oldest things on earth."

Then she kissed little Prince Ivan, and he climbed up on his big black horse, and leapt out of the window of the castle down on the end of the world, and galloped off on his way back over the wide world.

He came to Mountain-tosser, the giant. There was only one mountain left, and the giant was just picking it up. Sadly he was picking it up, for he knew that when he had thrown it away his work would be done and he would have to die.

"Well, little Prince Ivan," says Mountain-tosser, "this is the end;" and he heaves up the mountain. But before he could toss it away the little Prince threw his magic brush on the plain, and the brush swelled and burst, and there were range upon range of high mountains, touching the sky itself.

"Why," says Mountain-tosser, "I have enough mountains now to last me for another thousand years. Thank you kindly, little Prince."

And he set to work again, heaving up mountains and

tossing them down, while little Prince Ivan galloped on across the wide world.

He came to Tree-rooter, the giant. There were only two of the great oaks left, and the giant had one in each hand.

"Ah me, little Prince Ivan," says Tree-rooter, "my life is come to its end; for I have only to pluck up these two trees and throw them down, and then I shall die."

"Pluck them up," says little Prince Ivan. "Here are plenty more for you." And he threw down his comb. There was a noise of spreading branches, of swishing leaves, of opening buds, all together, and there before them was a forest of great oaks stretching farther than the giant could see, tall though he was.

"Why," says Tree-rooter, "here are enough trees to last me for another thousand years. Thank you kindly, little Prince."

And he set to work again, pulling up the big trees, laughing joyfully and hurling them over his head, while little Prince Ivan galloped on across the wide world.

He came to the two old women. They were crying their eyes out.

"There is only one needle left!" says the first.

"There is only one bit of thread in the box!" sobs the second.

"And then we shall die!" they say both together, mumbling with their old mouths.

"Before you use the needle and thread, just eat these apples," says little Prince Ivan, and he gives them the two apples of youth.

The two old women took the apples in their old shaking fingers and ate them, bent double, mumbling with their old lips. They had hardly finished their last mouthfuls when they sat up straight, smiled with sweet red lips, and looked at the little Prince with shining eyes. They had become young girls again, and their gray hair was black as the raven.

"Thank you kindly, little Prince," say the two young girls. "You must take with you the handkerchief we have been sewing all these years. Throw it to the ground, and it will turn into a lake of water. Perhaps some day it will be useful to you."

"Thank you," says the little Prince, and off he gallops, on and on over the wide world.

He came at last to his father's palace. The roof was gone, and there were holes in the walls. He left his horse at the edge of the garden, and crept up to the ruined palace and peeped through a hole. Inside, in the great hall, was sitting a huge baby girl, filling the whole hall. There was no room for her to move. She had knocked off the roof with a shake of her head. And she sat there in the ruined hall, sucking her thumb.

And while Prince Ivan was watching through the hole he heard her mutter to herself,—

> "Eaten the father, eaten the mother,
> And now to eat the little brother."

And she began shrinking, getting smaller and smaller every minute.

Little Prince Ivan had only just time to get away from the hole in the wall when a pretty little baby girl came running out of the ruined palace.

"You must be my little brother Ivan," she called out to him, and came up to him smiling. But as she smiled the little Prince saw that her teeth were black; and as she shut her mouth he heard them clink together like pokers.

"Come in," says she, and she took little Prince Ivan with her to a room in the palace, all broken down and cobwebbed. There was a dulcimer lying in the dust on the floor.

"Well, little brother," says the witch baby, "you play on the dulcimer and amuse yourself while I get supper ready. But don't stop playing, or I shall feel lonely." And she ran off and left him.

Little Prince Ivan sat down and played tunes on the dulcimer—sad enough tunes. You would not play dance music if you thought you were going to be eaten by a witch.

But while he was playing a little gray mouse came out of a crack in the floor. Some people think that this was the wise old groom, who had turned into a little gray mouse to save Ivan from the witch baby.

"Ivan, Ivan," says the little gray mouse, "run while you may. Your father and mother were eaten long ago, and well they deserved it. But be quick, or you will be eaten too. Your pretty little sister is putting an edge on her teeth!"

Little Prince Ivan thanked the mouse, and ran out from the ruined palace, and climbed up on the back of his big black horse, with its saddle and bridle trimmed with silver. Away he galloped over the wide world. The witch baby stopped her work and listened. She heard the music of the dulcimer, so she made sure he was still there. She went on sharpening her teeth with a file, and growing bigger and bigger every minute. And all the time the music of the dulcimer sounded among the ruins.

As soon as her teeth were quite sharp she rushed off to eat little Prince Ivan. She tore aside the walls of the room. There was nobody there—only a little gray mouse running and jumping this way and that on the strings of the dulcimer.

When it saw the witch baby the little mouse ran across the floor and into the crack and away, so that she never caught it. How the witch baby gnashed her teeth! Poker and tongs, poker and tongs—what a noise they made! She swelled up, bigger and bigger, till she was a baby as high as the palace. And then she jumped up so that the palace fell to pieces about her. Then off she ran after little Prince Ivan.

Little Prince Ivan, on the big black horse, heard a noise behind him. He looked back, and there was the huge witch, towering over the trees. She was dressed like a little baby, and her eyes flashed and her teeth clanged as she shut her mouth. She was running with long strides, faster even than the black horse could gallop—and he was the best horse in all the world.

Little Prince Ivan threw down the handkerchief that had been sewn by the two old women who had eaten the apples of youth. It turned into a deep, broad lake, so that the witch baby had to swim—and swimming is slower than running. It took her a long time to get across, and all that time Prince Ivan was galloping on, never stopping for a moment.

The witch baby crossed the lake and came thundering after him. Close behind she was, and would have caught him; but the giant Tree-rooter saw the little

Prince galloping on the big black horse, and the witch baby tearing after him. He pulled up the great oaks in armfuls, and threw them down just in front of the witch baby. He made a huge pile of the big trees, and the witch baby had to stop and gnaw her way through them with her iron teeth.

It took her a long time to gnaw through the trees, and the black horse galloped and galloped ahead. But presently Prince Ivan heard a noise behind him. He looked back, and there was the witch baby, thirty feet high, racing after him, clanging with her teeth. Close behind she was, and the little Prince sat firm on the big black horse, and galloped and galloped. But she would have caught him if the giant Mountain-tosser had not seen the little Prince on the big black horse, and the great witch baby running after him. The giant tore up the biggest mountain in the world and flung it down in front of her, and another on the top of that. She had to bite her way through them, while the little Prince galloped and galloped.

At last little Prince Ivan saw the cloud castle of the little sister of the Sun, hanging over the end of the world and gleaming in the sky as if it were made of roses. He shouted with hope, and the black horse shook his head proudly and galloped on. The witch baby thundered after him. Nearer she came and nearer.

"Ah, little one," screams the witch baby, "you shan't get away this time!"

The Sun's little sister was looking from a window of the castle in the sky, and she saw the witch baby stretching out to grab little Prince Ivan. She flung the window open, and just in time the big black horse leapt up, and through the window and into the courtyard, with little Prince Ivan safe on its back.

How the witch baby gnashed her iron teeth!

"Give him up!" she screams.

"I will not," says the Sun's little sister.

"See you here," says the witch baby, and she makes herself smaller and smaller and smaller, till she was just like a real little girl. "Let us be weighed in the great scales, and if I am heavier than Prince Ivan, I can take him; and if he is heavier than I am, I'll say no more about it."

The Sun's little sister laughed at the witch baby and teased her, and she hung the great scales out of the cloud castle so that they swung above the end of the world.

Little Prince Ivan got into one scale, and down it went.

"Now," says the witch baby, "we shall see."

And she made herself bigger and bigger and bigger, till she was as big as she had been when she sat and sucked her thumb in the hall of the ruined palace. "I am the heavier," she shouted, and gnashed her iron teeth. Then she jumped into the other scale.

She was so heavy that the scale with the little Prince in it shot up into the air. It shot up so fast that little Prince Ivan flew up into the sky, up and up and up, and came down on the topmost turret of the cloud castle of the little sister of the Sun.

The Sun's little sister laughed, and closed the window, and went up to the turret to meet the little Prince. But the witch baby turned back the way she had come, and went off, gnashing her iron teeth until they broke.

And ever since then, little Prince Ivan and the little sister of the Sun play together in the castle of cloud that hangs over the end of the world. They borrow the stars to play at ball, and put them back at night whenever they remember. And when there are no stars, it means that Prince Ivan and the Sun's little sister have gone to sleep over their games and forgotten to put their toys away.

The Firebird, the Horse of Power, and the Princess Vasilissa

ONCE UPON a time a strong and powerful Tzar ruled in a country far away. And among his servants was a young archer, and this archer had a horse—a horse of power—such a horse as belonged to the wonderful men of long ago—a great horse with a broad chest, eyes like fire, and hoofs of iron. There are no such horses nowadays. They sleep with the strong men who rode them, the bogatirs, until the time comes when Russia has need of them. Then the great horses will thunder up from under the ground, and the valiant men leap from the graves in the armour they have worn so long. The strong men will sit those horses of power, and there will be swinging of clubs and thunder of hoofs, and the earth will be swept clean from the enemies of God and the Tzar.

One day long ago, in the green time of the year, the young archer rode through the forest on his horse of power. The trees were green; there were little blue flowers on the ground under the trees; the squirrels ran in the branches, and the hares in the undergrowth; but no birds sang. The young archer rode along the forest path and listened for the singing of the birds, but there was no singing. The forest was silent, and the only noises in it were the scratching of four-footed beasts, the dropping of fir cones, and the heavy stamping of the horse of power in the soft path.

"What has come to the birds?" said the young archer.

He had scarcely said this before he saw a big curving feather lying in the path before him. The feather was larger than a swan's, larger than an eagle's. It lay in the path, glittering like a flame; for the sun was on it, and it was a feather of pure gold. Then he knew why there was no singing in the forest. For he knew that the firebird had flown that way, and that the feather in the path before him was a feather from its burning breast.

The horse of power spoke and said,—

"Leave the golden feather where it lies. If you take it you will be sorry for it, and know the meaning of fear."

But the brave young archer sat on the horse of power and looked at the golden feather, and wondered whether to take it or not. He had no wish to learn what it was to be afraid, but he thought, "If I take it and bring it to the Tzar my master, he will be pleased; and he will not send me away with empty hands, for no tzar in the world has a feather from the burning breast of the firebird." And the more he thought, the more he wanted to carry the feather to the Tzar. And in the end he did not listen to the words of the horse of power. He leapt from the saddle, picked up the golden feather of the firebird, mounted his horse again, and galloped back through the green forest till he came to the palace of the Tzar.

He went into the palace, and bowed before the Tzar and said,—

"O Tzar, I have brought you a feather of the firebird."

The Tzar looked gladly at the feather, and then at the young archer.

"Thank you," says he; "but if you have brought me a feather of the firebird, you will be able to bring me the bird itself. I should like to see it. A feather is not a fit gift to bring to the Tzar. Bring the bird itself, or, I swear by my sword, your head shall no longer sit between your shoulders!"

The young archer bowed his head and went out. Bitterly he wept, for he knew now what it was to be afraid. He went out into the courtyard, where the horse of power was waiting for him, tossing its head and stamping on the ground.

"Master," says the horse of power, "why do you weep?"

"The Tzar has told me to bring him the firebird, and no man on earth can do that," says the young archer, and he bowed his head on his breast.

"I told you," says the horse of power, "that if you took the feather you would learn the meaning of fear. Well, do not be frightened yet, and do not weep. The trouble is not now; the trouble lies before you. Go to the Tzar and ask him to have a hundred sacks of maize scattered over the open field, and let this be done at midnight."

The young archer went back into the palace and begged the Tzar for this, and the Tzar ordered that at midnight a hundred sacks of maize should be scattered in the open field.

Next morning, at the first redness in the sky, the young archer rode out on the horse of power, and came to the open field. The ground was scattered all over with maize. In the middle of the field stood a great oak with spreading boughs. The young archer leapt to the ground, took off the saddle, and let the horse of power loose to wander as he pleased about the field. Then he climbed up into the oak and hid himself among the green boughs.

The sky grew red and gold, and the sun rose. Suddenly there was a noise in the forest round the field. The trees shook and swayed, and almost fell. There was a mighty wind. The sea piled itself into waves with crests of foam, and the firebird came flying from the other side of the world. Huge and golden and flaming in the sun, it flew, dropped down with open wings into the field, and began to eat the maize.

The horse of power wandered in the field. This way he went, and that, but always he came a little nearer to the firebird. Nearer and nearer came the horse. He came close up to the firebird, and then suddenly stepped on one of its spreading fiery wings and pressed it heavily to the ground. The bird struggled, flapping mightily with its fiery wings, but it could not get away. The young archer slipped down from the tree, bound the firebird with three strong ropes, swung it on his back, saddled the horse, and rode to the palace of the Tzar.

The young archer stood before the Tzar, and his back was bent under the great weight of the firebird, and the broad wings of the bird hung on either side of him like fiery shields, and there was a trail of golden feathers on the floor. The young archer swung the magic bird to the foot of the throne before the Tzar; and the Tzar was glad, because since the beginning of the world no tzar had seen the firebird flung before him like a wild duck caught in a snare.

He came close up to the firebird, and then suddenly stepped
on one of its spreading fiery wings.

The Tzar looked at the firebird and laughed with pride. Then he lifted his eyes and looked at the young archer, and says he,—

"As you have known how to take the firebird, you will know how to bring me my bride, for whom I have long been waiting. In the land of Never, on the very edge of the world, where the red sun rises in flame from behind the sea, lives the Princess Vasilissa. I will marry none but her. Bring her to me, and I will reward you with silver and gold. But if you do not bring her, then, by my sword, your head will no longer sit between your shoulders!"

The young archer wept bitter tears, and went out into the courtyard, where the horse of power was stamping the ground with its hoofs of iron and tossing its thick mane.

"Master, why do you weep?" asked the horse of power.

"The Tzar has ordered me to go to the land of Never, and to bring back the Princess Vasilissa."

"Do not weep—do not grieve. The trouble is not yet; the trouble is to come. Go to the Tzar and ask him for a silver tent with a golden roof, and for all kinds of food and drink to take with us on the journey."

The young archer went in and asked the Tzar for this, and the Tzar gave him a silver tent with silver hangings and a gold-embroidered roof, and every kind of rich wine and the tastiest of foods.

Then the young archer mounted the horse of power and rode off to the land of Never. On and on he rode, many days and nights, and came at last to the edge of the world, where the red sun rises in flame from behind the deep blue sea.

On the shore of the sea the young archer reined in the horse of power, and the heavy hoofs of the horse sank in the sand. He shaded his eyes and looked out over the blue water, and there was the Princess Vasilissa in a little silver boat, rowing with golden oars.

The young archer rode back a little way to where the sand ended and the green world began. There he loosed the horse to wander where he pleased, and to feed on the green grass. Then on the edge of the shore, where the green grass ended and grew thin and the sand began, he set up the shining tent, with its silver hangings and its gold-embroidered roof. In the tent he set out the tasty dishes and the rich flagons of wine which the Tzar had given him, and he sat himself down in the tent and began to regale himself, while he waited for the Princess Vasilissa.

The Princess Vasilissa dipped her golden oars in the blue water, and the little silver boat moved lightly through the dancing waves. She sat in the little boat and looked over the blue sea to the edge of the world, and there, between the golden sand and the green earth, she saw the tent standing, silver and gold in the sun. She dipped her oars, and came nearer to see it the better. The nearer she came the fairer seemed the tent, and at last she rowed to the shore and grounded her little boat on the golden sand, and stepped out daintily and came up to the tent. She was a little frightened, and now and again she stopped and looked back to where the silver boat lay on the sand with the blue sea beyond it. The young archer said not a word, but went on regaling himself on the pleasant dishes he had set out there in the tent.

At last the Princess Vasilissa came up to the tent and looked in.

The young archer rose and bowed before her. Says he,—

"Good-day to you, Princess! Be so kind as to come in and take bread and salt with me, and taste my foreign wines."

And the Princess Vasilissa came into the tent and sat down with the young archer, and ate sweetmeats with him, and drank his health in a golden goblet of the wine the Tzar had given him. Now this wine was heavy, and the last drop from the goblet had no sooner trickled down her little slender throat than her eyes closed against her will, once, twice, and again.

"Ah me!" says the Princess, "it is as if the night itself had perched on my eyelids, and yet it is but noon."

And the golden goblet dropped to the ground from her little fingers, and she leant back on a cushion and fell instantly asleep. If she had been beautiful before, she was lovelier still when she lay in that deep sleep in the shadow of the tent.

Quickly the young archer called to the horse of power. Lightly he lifted the Princess in his strong young arms. Swiftly he leapt with her into the saddle. Like a feather she lay in the hollow of his left arm, and slept while the iron hoofs of the great horse thundered over the ground.

They came to the Tzar's palace, and the young archer leapt from the horse of power and carried the Princess into the palace. Great was the joy of the Tzar; but it did not last for long.

"Go, sound the trumpets for our wedding," he said to his servants; "let all the bells be rung."

The bells rang out and the trumpets sounded, and at the noise of the horns and the ringing of the bells the Princess Vasilissa woke up and looked about her.

"What is this ringing of bells," says she, "and this noise of trumpets? And where, oh, where is the blue sea, and my little silver boat with its golden oars?" And the Princess put her hand to her eyes.

"The blue sea is far away," says the Tzar, "and for your little silver boat I give you a golden throne. The trumpets sound for our wedding, and the bells are ringing for our joy."

But the Princess turned her face away from the Tzar; and there was no wonder in that, for he was old, and his eyes were not kind.

And she looked with love at the young archer; and there was no wonder in that either, for he was a young man fit to ride the horse of power.

The Tzar was angry with the Princess Vasilissa, but his anger was as useless as his joy.

"Why, Princess," says he, "will you not marry me, and forget your blue sea and your silver boat?"

"In the middle of the deep blue sea lies a great stone," says the Princess, "and under that stone is hidden my wedding dress. If I cannot wear that dress I will marry nobody at all."

Instantly the Tzar turned to the young archer, who was waiting before the throne.

"Ride swiftly back," says he, "to the land of Never, where the red sun rises in flame. There—do you hear what the Princess says?—a great stone lies in the middle of the sea. Under that stone is hidden her wedding dress. Ride swiftly. Bring back that dress, or, by my sword, your head shall no longer sit between your shoulders!"

The young archer wept bitter tears, and went out into the courtyard, where the horse of power was waiting for him, champing its golden bit.

"There is no way of escaping death this time," he said.

"Master, why do you weep?" asked the horse of power.

"The Tzar has ordered me to ride to the land of Never, to fetch the wedding dress of the Princess Vasilissa from the bottom of the deep blue sea. Besides, the dress is wanted for the Tzar's wedding, and I love the Princess myself."

"What did I tell you?" says the horse of power. "I told you that there would be trouble if you picked up the golden feather from the firebird's burning breast. Well, do not be afraid. The trouble is not yet; the trouble is to come. Up! into the saddle with you, and away for the wedding dress of the Princess Vasilissa!"

The young archer leapt into the saddle, and the horse of power, with his thundering hoofs, carried him swiftly through the green forests and over the bare plains, till they came to the edge of the world, to the land of Never, where the red sun rises in flame from behind the deep blue sea. There they rested, at the very edge of the sea.

The young archer looked sadly over the wide waters, but the horse of power tossed its mane and did not look at the sea, but on the shore. This way and that it looked, and saw at last a huge lobster moving slowly, sideways, along the golden sand.

Nearer and nearer came the lobster, and it was a

giant among lobsters, the tzar of all the lobsters; and it moved slowly along the shore, while the horse of power moved carefully and as if by accident, until it stood between the lobster and the sea. Then, when the lobster came close by, the horse of power lifted an iron hoof and set it firmly on the lobster's tail.

"You will be the death of me!" screamed the lobster—as well he might, with the heavy foot of the horse of power pressing his tail into the sand. "Let me live, and I will do whatever you ask of me."

"Very well," says the horse of power; "we will let you live," and he slowly lifted his foot. "But this is what you shall do for us. In the middle of the blue sea lies a great stone, and under that stone is hidden the wedding dress of the Princess Vasilissa. Bring it here."

The lobster groaned with the pain in his tail. Then he cried out in a voice that could be heard all over the deep blue sea. And the sea was disturbed, and from all sides lobsters in thousands made their way towards the bank. And the huge lobster that was the oldest of them all and the tzar of all the lobsters that live between the rising and the setting of the sun, gave them the order and sent them back into the sea. And the young archer sat on the horse of power and waited.

After a little time the sea was disturbed again, and the lobsters in their thousands came to the shore, and with them they brought a golden casket in which was the wedding dress of the Princess Vasilissa. They had taken it from under the great stone that lay in the middle of the sea.

The tzar of all the lobsters raised himself painfully on his bruised tail and gave the casket into the hands of the young archer, and instantly the horse of power turned himself about and galloped back to the palace of the Tzar, far, far away, at the other side of the green forests and beyond the treeless plains.

The young archer went into the palace and gave the casket into the hands of the Princess, and looked at her with sadness in his eyes, and she looked at him with love. Then she went away into an inner chamber, and came back in her wedding dress, fairer than the spring itself. Great was the joy of the Tzar. The wedding feast was made ready, and the bells rang, and flags waved above the palace.

The Tzar held out his hand to the Princess, and looked at her with his old eyes. But she would not take his hand.

"No," says she; "I will marry nobody until the man who brought me here has done penance in boiling water."

Instantly the Tzar turned to his servants and ordered them to make a great fire, and to fill a great cauldron with water and set it on the fire, and, when the water should be at its hottest, to take the young archer and throw him into it, to do penance for having taken the Princess Vasilissa away from the land of Never.

There was no gratitude in the mind of that Tzar.

Swiftly the servants brought wood and made a mighty fire, and on it they laid a huge cauldron of water, and built the fire round the walls of the cauldron. The fire burned hot and the water steamed. The fire burned hotter, and the water bubbled and seethed. They made ready to take the young archer, to throw him into the cauldron.

"Oh, misery!" thought the young archer. "Why did I

ever take the golden feather that had fallen from the firebird's burning breast? Why did I not listen to the wise words of the horse of power?" And he remembered the horse of power, and he begged the Tzar,—

"O lord Tzar, I do not complain. I shall presently die in the heat of the water on the fire. Suffer me, before I die, once more to see my horse."

"Let him see his horse," says the Princess.

"Very well," says the Tzar. "Say good-bye to your horse, for you will not ride him again. But let your farewells be short, for we are waiting."

The young archer crossed the courtyard and came to the horse of power, who was scraping the ground with his iron hoofs.

"Farewell, my horse of power," says the young archer. "I should have listened to your words of wisdom, for now the end is come, and we shall never more see the green trees pass above us and the ground disappear beneath us, as we race the wind between the earth and the sky."

"Why so?" says the horse of power.

"The Tzar has ordered that I am to be boiled to death—thrown into that cauldron that is seething on the great fire."

"Fear not," says the horse of power, "for the Princess Vasilissa has made him do this, and the end of these things is better than I thought. Go back, and when they are ready to throw you in the cauldron, do you run boldly and leap yourself into the boiling water."

The young archer went back across the courtyard, and the servants made ready to throw him into the cauldron.

"Are you sure that the water is boiling?" says the Princess Vasilissa.

"It bubbles and seethes," said the servants.

"Let me see for myself," says the Princess, and she went to the fire and waved her hand above the cauldron. And some say there was something in her hand, and some say there was not.

"It is boiling," says she, and the servants laid hands on the young archer; but he threw them from him, and ran and leapt boldly before them all into the very middle of the cauldron.

Twice he sank below the surface, borne round with the bubbles and foam of the boiling water. Then he leapt from the cauldron and stood before the Tzar and the Princess. He had become so beautiful a youth that all who saw cried aloud in wonder.

"This is a miracle," says the Tzar. And the Tzar looked at the beautiful young archer, and thought of himself—of his age, of his bent back, and his gray beard, and his toothless gums. "I too will become beautiful," thinks he, and he rose from his throne and clambered into the cauldron, and was boiled to death in a moment.

And the end of the story? They buried the Tzar, and made the young archer Tzar in his place. He married the Princess Vasilissa, and lived many years with her in love and good fellowship. And he built a golden stable for the horse of power, and never forgot what he owed to him.